"Your battery is dead." Caveman glanced around. "You got another handy?"

She shook her head. "No. Fresh out."

"Got a helmet?"

She nodded. "Yeah, but I won't need it if I can't get my ATV started."

He spun and headed for the barn door. "You can ride on the back of mine," he called out over his shoulder.

Grace's heart fluttered at the thought of riding behind Caveman, holding him around the waist to keep from falling off. "No, thanks. Those trails are dangerous." She suspected the danger was more in how her pulse quickened around the man than the possibility of plunging over the edge of a drop-off.

"I grew up riding horses and four-wheelers on rugged mountain trails. I won't let you fall off a cliff." He held up a hand. "Promise."

She frowned. Knowing she only had a few minutes to get to the meeting location, Grace sighed. "Okay. I guess I'll put my life in your hands." She followed him out of the barn and closed the door behind her. "Although, I don't know why I should trust you. I don't even know you."

HOT TARGET

New York Times Bestselling Author
ELLE JAMES

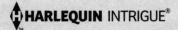 HARLEQUIN INTRIGUE®

This book is dedicated to my mother and father,
who taught me that the sky was the limit, and all I needed
was to apply the hard work to reach for my dreams.
I love you both to the moon and back.

ISBN-13: 978-0-373-75662-9

Recycling programs
for this product may
not exist in your area.

Hot Target

Copyright © 2017 by Mary Jernigan

Printed in U.S.A.

www.Harlequin.com

Elle James, a *New York Times* bestselling author, started writing when her sister challenged her to write a romance novel. She has managed a full-time job and raised three wonderful children, and she and her husband even tried ranching exotic birds (ostriches, emus and rheas). Ask her, and she'll tell you what it's like to go toe-to-toe with an angry 350-pound bird! Elle loves to hear from fans at ellejames@earthlink.net or ellejames.com.

Books by Elle James

Harlequin Intrigue

Ballistic Cowboys

Hot Combat
Hot Target

SEAL of My Own

Navy SEAL Survival
Navy SEAL Captive
Navy SEAL to Die For
Navy SEAL Six Pack

Covert Cowboys, Inc.

Triggered
Taking Aim
Bodyguard Under Fire
Cowboy Resurrected
Navy SEAL Justice
Navy SEAL Newlywed
High Country Hideout
Clandestine Christmas

Visit the Author Profile page at Harlequin.com for more titles.

CAST OF CHARACTERS

Max "Caveman" Decker—US Army DELTA Force soldier on loan to the Department of Homeland Security for Task Force Safe Haven.

Grace Saunders—Biologist working on the Wolf Project with Yellowstone National Park. Witnessed a murder, thus becoming a target of the killer.

Kevin Garner—Agent with the Department of Homeland Security in charge of Task Force Safe Haven.

Jon "Ghost" Caspar—US Navy SEAL on loan to Department of Homeland Security for Task Force Safe Haven, a special group of military men assigned to Homeland Security.

Tarce "Hawkeye" Walsh—US Army Airborne Ranger and expert sniper, on loan to the Department of Homeland Security for Task Force Safe Haven.

Rex "T-Rex" Trainor—US Marine on loan to the Department of Homeland Security for Task Force Safe Haven.

Ernie Martin—Rancher angry about cessation of government subsidies on his Angora goat ranching business.

Quincy Kemp—Local meat processor and taxidermist.

Bryson Rausch—Formerly the wealthiest resident of Grizzly Pass, who lost everything in the stock market.

RJ Khalig—Pipeline inspector who replaced previous one who had been giving false reports.

Chapter One

Max "Caveman" Decker clung to the shadows of the mud-and-brick structures, the first SEAL into enemy territory. Reaching a forward position giving him sufficient range of fire, he dropped to one knee, scanned the street and buildings ahead through his night-vision goggles, searching for the telltale green heat signatures of warm enemy bodies. When he didn't detect any, he said softly into his mic, "Ready."

"Going in," Whiskey said. Armed with their M4A1 carbine rifles with the Special Forces Modification kit, he and Tank eased around the corner of a building in a small village in the troubled Helmand Province of Afghanistan.

Army Intelligence operatives had indicated the Pakistan-based Haqqani followers had set *up a remote base of operations in the village located in the rugged hills north of Kandahar.*

Caveman's job was to provide cover to his teammates as they moved ahead of him. Then they would cover for him until he reached a relatively secure location, thus leapfrogging through the village to their target, the biggest building at the center, where intel reported the Haqqani rebels had set up shop.

Caveman hunkered low, scanning the path ahead and the rooftops of the buildings for gun-toting enemy combatants. So far, so good. Through his night-vision goggles, he tracked the progress of the seven members of his squad working their way slowly toward the target.

An eighth green blip appeared ahead of his team and his arm swung wide.

"We've got incoming!" Caveman aimed his weapon at the eighth green heat signature and pulled the trigger. It was too late. A bright flash blinded him through the goggles, followed by the ear-rupturing concussion of a grenade. He jerked his goggles up over his helmet, cursing. When he blinked his eyes to regain his night vision, he stared at the scene in front of him.

All seven members of his squad lay on the ground, some moving, others not.

No! His job was to provide cover. They couldn't be dead. They had to be alive. He leaped to his feet.

Then, as if someone opened the door to a hive of bees, enemy combatants swarmed from around the corners into the street, carrying AK-47s.

With the majority of his squad down, maybe dead, maybe alive, Caveman didn't have any other choice.

He set his weapon on automatic, pulled his 9-millimeter pistol from the holster on his hip and stepped out of the cover of the building.

"What the hell are you doing?" Whiskey had shouted.

"Showing no mercy," he shouted through gritted teeth. He charged forward like John Wayne on the warpath, shooting from both hips, taking out one enemy rebel after the other.

Something hit him square in his armor-plated chest, knocking him backward a step. It hurt like hell and made his breath lodge in his lungs, but it didn't stop him. He forged his way toward the enemy, firing until he ran out of ammo. Dropping to the ground, he slammed magazines into the rifle and the pistol and rolled to a prone position, aimed and fired, taking down as many of the enemy as he could. He'd be damned if even one of them survived.

When there were only two combatants left in the street, Caveman lurched to his feet and went after them. He wouldn't rest until the last one died.

He hadn't slowed as he rounded the corner. A bullet had hit him in the leg. Caveman grunted. He would have gone down, but the adrenaline in his veins surged, pushing him to his destination. He aimed his pistol at the shooter who'd plugged his leg and caught him between the eyes. Another bogey shot at him from above.

Caveman dove to the ground and rolled behind a stack of crates. Pain stabbed him in the shoulder and the leg, and warm wetness dripped down both. He leaned around the crates, pulled his night-vision goggles in place, located the shooter on the rooftop and took him out.

With the streets clear, he had a straight path to the original target. Holstering his handgun, he pulled a grenade out of his vest, pushed to his feet and staggered a few steps, pain slicing through him. He could barely feel his leg and really didn't give a damn.

Two steps, three... One after the other took him to the biggest structure in the neighborhood. As he rounded the corner, one of the two guards protecting the doorway fired at him.

The man's bullet hit the stucco beside him.

Caveman jerked back behind the corner, stuck his M4A1 around the corner and fired off a burst. Then he leaped out, threw himself to the ground, rolled and came up firing. Within moments, the two guards were dead.

The door was locked or barred from the inside. Pulling the pin on the grenade, Caveman dropped it in front of the barrier and then stepped back around the corner, covering his ears.

The blast shook the building and spewed dust and wooden splinters. Back at the front entrance, Caveman kicked the door the rest of the way in and entered the building.

Going from room to room, he fired his weapon, taking out every male occupant in his path. When he reached the last door, he kicked it open and stood back.

The expected gunfire riddled the wall opposite the door.

After the gunfire ceased, Caveman spun around and opened fire on the occupants of the room until no one stood or attempted escape.

His task complete, he radioed the platoon leader. "Eight down. Come get us." Only after each one of his enemies was dead did he allow himself to crumple to the ground. As if every bone in his body suddenly melted into goo, Caveman had no way left to hold himself up. Still armed with his M4A1, he sat in the big room and stared down at his leg. Blood flowed far too quickly. In the back of his mind, he knew he had to do something or he'd pass out and die. But every movement now took a monumental amount of effort, and gray fog gathered at the edges of his vision. He couldn't pass out now, his buddies needed him. They could be dead or dying. No matter how hard he tried, he couldn't straighten, couldn't rise to his feet. The abyss claimed him, dragging him to the depths of despair.

"CAVEMAN," A VOICE SAID.

He dragged himself back from the edge

of a very dark, extremely deep pool that was his past—a different time…a terrible place. He shook his head to clear the memories and glanced across the room at his new boss for the duration of this temporary assignment. "I'm sorry, sir. You were saying?"

The leader of Homeland Security's Special Task Force Safe Haven, Kevin Garner, narrowed his eyes. "How long did you say it's been since you were cleared for duty?"

"Two weeks," Caveman responded.

Kevin's frown deepened. "And when was the last time you met with a shrink?"

"All through the twelve weeks of physical therapy. She cleared me two weeks ago." His jaw tightened. "I'm fully capable of performing whatever assignment is given to me as a Delta Force soldier. I don't know why I've been assigned to this backcountry boondoggle."

Kevin's shrewd gaze studied Caveman so hard he could have been staring at him under a microscope. "Any TBI with your injury?"

"I was shot in the leg, not the head. No traumatic brain injury." Anger spiked with the need to get outside and breathe fresh air. Not that the air in the loft over the Blue Moose Tavern in Grizzly Pass, Wyoming, was stale. It was just that whenever Caveman was inside for extended periods, he got really twitchy. Claustrophobia, the therapist had called it. Probably brought on by PTSD.

A bunch of hooey, if you asked Caveman. Something the therapist could use against him to delay his return to the front. And by God, he'd get back to the front soon, if he had to stow away on a C-130 bound for Afghanistan. The enemy had to pay for the deaths of his friends; the members of his squad deserved retribution. Only one other man had survived, Whiskey, and he'd lost an eye in the firefight.

The slapping sound of a file folder hitting a tabletop made Caveman jump.

"That's your assignment," Kevin said. "RJ Khalig, pipeline inspector. He's had a few threats lately. I want you to touch bases with him and provide protection until we can figure out who's threatening him."

Caveman glared at the file. "I'm no bodyguard. I shoot people for a living."

"You know the stakes from our meeting a couple days ago in this same room, and you've seen what some of the people in this area are capable of. As I said then, we think terrorist cells are stirring up already volatile locals. Since we found evidence that someone is supplying semiautomatic weapons to what we suspect is a local group called Free America, we're afraid more violence is imminent."

"Just because you found some empty crates in that old mine doesn't mean whoever got the weapons plans to use them to start a war," Caveman argued.

"No, but we're concerned they might target individuals who could potentially stand in the way of their movements."

"Why not let local law enforcement handle it?" Caveman leaned forward, reluctant to open the file and commit to the assignment. He didn't want to be in Wyoming. "If this group picks off individuals, would that not be local jurisdiction?"

Kevin nodded. "As long as they aren't connected with terrorists. However, the activity on social media indicates something bigger is being planned and will take place soon."

"How soon?"

Kevin shook his head. "We don't know."

"Sounds pretty vague to me." Caveman stood and stretched.

"I set up this task force to stop a terrible thing from happening. If I had all of the answers, likely I wouldn't need you, Ghost, Hawkeye or T-Rex. I'm determined to stop something bad from happening, before it gets too big and a lot more lives are lost."

"I don't know if you have the right guy for this job. I'm no investigator, nor am I a bodyguard."

"I understand your concern, but we need trained combatants, familiar with tactics and subversive operations. As you've seen for yourself and know from experience, it's pretty rough country out here and the people can be stubborn and willing to take the law into their own hands. I'm afraid what happened at the mine two days ago could happen again."

Caveman snorted. "That was a bunch of disgruntled ranchers, mad about the confiscation of their herd."

"Agreed," Kevin said. "Granted, the Vanders family took it too far by kidnapping a busload of kids. But they knew about the weapons stored in that mine."

"Are any of them talking?"

"Not yet. We're waiting for one of them to throw the rest under the bus."

"You might be waiting a long time." Caveman crossed his arms over his chest. "People out here tend to be very stubborn."

"You're from this area," Kevin said. "You should know."

"I'm from a little farther north, in the Crazy Mountains of Montana. But we're all a tough bunch of cowboys who don't like it when the government interferes with our lives."

"Hold on to that stubbornness. You might need it around here. For today, you'll be an investigator and bodyguard. Mr. Khalig needs your help. He has an important job, inspecting the oil and gas pipelines running through this state. Contact his boss for his location, find him and get the skinny on what's going on. You might have to run him down in the backwoods."

Until he was cleared to return to his unit, Caveman would do the best he could for his temporary boss and the pipeline inspector. What choice did he have? As much as he hated to admit it, they needed help out in the hills and mountains of Wyoming. The three days he'd been there had proven that.

Caveman had met with Kevin's four-man special operations team members. One Navy

SEAL, one Delta Force soldier, an Army ranger and a highly skilled Marine. Ghost, one of the Delta Force men, had been assigned to protect a woman who had been surfing the web for terrorist activity. Her daughter had been one of the children who had been kidnapped on the bus.

Caveman, Kevin and the other three members of the task force had mobilized to save the children and the three adults on board the bus. The bus driver didn't make it, but the children and the two women survived.

Kevin stood and held out his hand. "Thanks for helping out. We have such limited resources in this neck of the woods, and I feel there's a lot more to what's going on here than meets the eyes."

"I'll do what I can." Caveman shook Kevin's hand and left the loft, descending the stairs to the street below. When he'd entered the upstairs apartment, the sky had been clear and blue. In the twenty minutes he'd been inside, clouds had gathered. The superstitious would call it an omen, a sign or a portent of things to come. Caveman called them rain clouds. If he was going to get out to where Khalig was, he'd have to get moving.

GRACE SAUNDERS PULLED her horse to a halt and dismounted near the top of a ridge overlooking the mountain meadow where Molly's wolf pack had been spotted most recently. Based on the droppings she'd seen along the trail and the leftover bones of an elk carcass, they were still active in the area.

She tied her horse to a nearby tree and stretched her back and legs. Having been on horseback since early that morning, she was ready for a break. Moving to the highest point, she stared out at the brilliant view of the Wyoming Beartooth Mountain Range, with the snowcapped peaks and the tall lodgepole pines. The sky above had been blue when she'd started her trek that morning. Clouds had built to the west, a harbinger of rain to come soon. She'd have to head down soon or risk a cold drenching.

From where she stood, Grace could see clear across the small valley to the hilltop on the other side. She frowned, squinted her eyes and focused on something that didn't belong.

A four-wheeler stood at the top of the hill, halfway tucked into the shade of a lodgepole pine tree. She wondered what someone else was doing out in the woods. Most people stuck to the roads in and out of the national forest.

It wasn't unusual for the more adventurous souls to ride the trails surrounding Yellowstone National Park, since ATVs in the park itself were prohibited. Scanning the hilltop for the person belonging to the four-wheeler, Grace had to search hard. For a moment she worried the rider might be hurt. Then she spotted him, lying on his belly on the ground.

Grace's heartbeats ratcheted up several notches. The guy appeared to have a rifle of some sort with a scope. Since it was summer, the man with the gun had no reason to be aiming a rifle. It wasn't hunting season.

Grace followed the direction the barrel of the weapon was pointed, to the far side of the valley. She couldn't see any elk, white-tailed deer or moose. Was he aiming for wolves? Grace raised her binoculars to her eyes and looked closer.

A movement caught her attention. She almost missed it. But then she focused on the spot where she'd seen the movement and gasped.

A man squatted near the ground with a device in his hand. He stared at the device as he slowly stood.

Grace shifted the lenses of her binoculars to the man on the ridge. He tensed, his eye lining up with the scope. Surely he wasn't aiming at the man on the ground.

Her pulse hammering, Grace lowered her binoculars and shouted to the man below. "Get down!"

At the same time as she shouted, the sound of rifle fire reached her.

The man on the floor of the valley jerked, pressed a hand to his chest and looked down at blood spreading across his shirt. He dropped to his knees and then fell forward.

Grace pressed a hand to her chest, her heart hammering against her ribs. What had just happened? In her heart she knew. She'd just witnessed a murder. Raising her binoculars to the man on the hilltop, she stared at him, trying to get a good look at him so that she could pick him out in a lineup of criminals.

He had brown hair. And that was all she could get before she noticed the gun he'd used to kill the man on the valley floor was pointing in her direction, and he was aiming at her.

Instinctively, Grace dropped to the ground

and rolled to the side. Dust kicked up at the point she'd been standing a moment before. The rifle's report sounded half a second later.

Grace rolled again until she was below the top of the ridge. Afraid to stand and risk being shot, she crawled on all fours down to where she'd left her horse tied to a tree.

An engine revved on the other side of the ridge, the sound echoing off the rocky bluffs.

Her pulse slamming through her body, Grace staggered to her feet, her knees shaking. She ran toward the horse. The animal backed away, sensing her distress, pulling the knot tighter on the tree branch.

Her hands trembling, Grace struggled to untie the knot.

Tears stung her eyes. She wanted to go back to the man on the ground and see if he was still alive, but the shooter would take her out before she could get there. Her best bet was to get back down the mountain and notify the sheriff. If she rode hard, she could be down in thirty minutes.

Finally jerking the reins free of the branch, Grace swung up onto the horse.

The gelding leaped forward as soon as her

butt hit the saddle, galloping down the trail they'd climbed moments before.

Grace slowed as she approached a point at which the trail narrowed and dropped off on one side. With the gelding straining at the bit to speed up, Grace held him in check as they eased down the trail. She glanced back at the ridge where she'd been. A four-wheeler stood on top, the rider holding a rifle to his shoulder.

Something hit the bluff beside her. Dust and rocks splintered off, blinding her briefly. Throwing caution to the wind, she gave the horse his head and held on, praying they didn't fall off the side of the trail. She didn't have a choice. If she didn't get around the corner soon, she'd be shot.

Her gelding pushed forward, more sure of his footing than Grace. She ducked low in the saddle and held on, praying they made it soon. The bluff jutted out of the hillside and would provide sufficient cover for a few minutes. Long enough for her to make it to the trees. The shooter could still catch up, but the trail twisting through the thick trunks of the evergreens would give her more cover and concealment than being in the open. If she made it down to the paved road, she could wave someone down.

Riding like her hair was on fire, Grace erupted from the trees at the base of the mountain trail. A truck with a trailer on the back was parked on the dirt road. She slowed to read the sign on the door, indicating Rocky Mountain Pipeline Inc. No sooner had she stopped than a shot rang out, plinking into the side of the truck.

Grace leaned low over her horse and yelled, "Go, go, go!" The horse took off across a field, galloping hard.

Then, as if he tripped, he stumbled and pitched forward.

Grace sailed through the air, every move appearing in slow motion. She made a complete somersault before she landed on her feet. Momentum carried her forward and she landed hard on her belly in the tall grass, her forehead bumping the ground hard. For a moment, she couldn't breathe and her vision blurred. She knew she couldn't stay there. The guy on the four-wheeler would catch up to her and finish the job.

An engine roared somewhere nearby.

Grace low-crawled through the grass, blinking hard to clear the darkness slowing her down. When she could go no farther, she collapsed in the grass, no longer able to fight against the fog closing in around her. She closed her eyes.

It wouldn't take the gunman long to find her and end it.

Then she felt a hand on her shoulder and heard a man calling to her as if from the far end of a long tunnel.

"Hey, are you all right?" a deep, resonant voice called out.

Grace gave the last bit of her strength to pushing herself over onto her back. She made it halfway and groaned.

The hand on her shoulder eased her the rest of the way, until she lay facing her attacker. "Are you going to kill me?"

"What?" he said. "Why would I want to kill you?"

"You killed the man in the valley. And you tried to kill me," she said, her voice fading into a whisper.

"I'm not here to kill anyone."

"If you do. Just make it quick." She tried to

blink her eyes open, but they wouldn't move. "Just shoot me. But don't hurt my horse." And she passed out.

Chapter Two

Caveman shook his head as he stared down at the strange woman. "Shoot you? I don't even know you," he muttered. He glanced around, searching for others in the area. She had to have a reason to think he was there to kill her.

He ran his gaze over her body, searching for wounds. Other than the bump on her forehead, she appeared to be okay, despite being tossed by her horse.

The animal had recovered his footing and taken off toward the highway.

Caveman would have the sheriff come out and retrieve the horse. For now, the woman needed to be taken to the hospital. He ran back to his truck for his cell phone, knowing the chances it would work out there were slim to none. But he had to try. He checked. No service.

How the heck was he supposed to call for an airlift? Then he remembered where he was. The foothills of the Beartooth Mountains. He didn't have the radio communications he was used to, or the helicopter support to bring injured teammates out of a bad situation.

With no other choice, he threw open the truck's rear door, returned to the woman, scooped her up in his arms and carried her to his truck. Carefully laying her on the backseat, he buckled a seat belt around her hips and stared down at her. Just to make certain she was still alive, he checked for a pulse.

Still beating. *Good.*

She had straight, sandy-blond hair, clear, makeup-free skin and appeared to be somewhere between twenty-five and thirty years old. The spill she'd taken from her horse could have caused a head, neck or back injury. If they weren't in the mountains, where bears, wolves and other animals could find her, he would have left her lying still until a medic could bring a backboard, to avoid further injury. But out in the open, with wolves and grizzlies a real threat, Caveman couldn't leave the woman.

He shut the door and climbed into the driver's seat. The man he was supposed to meet out there would have to wait. This woman needed immediate medical attention.

As soon as he got closer to the little town of Grizzly Pass, he checked his phone for service. He had enough to get a call through to Kevin Garner. "Caveman here. I have an injured woman in the backseat of my truck. I'm taking her to the local clinic. You'll have to send someone else out to meet with Mr. Khalig. I don't know when I'll get back out there."

"Who've you got?" Kevin asked.

"I don't know. She was thrown from the horse she was riding. She hasn't been conscious long enough to tell me her life history, much less her name."

"Grace," a gravelly voice said from the backseat.

Caveman glanced over his shoulder.

"My name's Grace Saunders." The woman he'd settled on the backseat pushed to a sitting position and pressed a hand to the back of her head. "Who are you? Where am I?"

"I take it she's awake?" Kevin said into Caveman's ear.

"Roger." He shot a glance at the rearview mirror, into the soft gray eyes of the woman he'd rescued. "Gotta go, Kevin. Will update you as soon as I know anything."

"I'll see if I can find someone I can send out to check on Mr. Khalig," Kevin said.

His gaze moving from the road ahead to the reflection of the woman behind him, Caveman focused on Kevin's words. "I found a truck and trailer where his office staff said it would be, but the man himself wasn't anywhere nearby."

"I suspect that truck and trailer either belong to the dead man or the man who was doing the shooting," the woman in the backseat said.

"Dead man?" Caveman removed his foot from the accelerator. "What dead man? What shooting?"

"I'll tell you when we get to town. Right now my head hurts." She touched the lump on her forehead and winced. "Where are we going?"

He didn't demand to know what she was talking about, knowing the woman needed medical attention after her fall. "To the clinic in Grizzly Pass." He'd get the full story once she had been checked out.

"I don't need to go to the clinic." She leaned over the back of the seat and touched his shoulder. "Take me to the sheriff's office."

Caveman frowned. "Lady, you need to see a doctor. You were out cold."

"My name is Grace, and I know what I need. And that's to see the sheriff. *Now*."

He glanced at her face in the mirror. "Okay, but if you pass out, I'm taking you to the clinic. No argument."

"Deal." She nodded toward the road ahead. "You'd better slow down or you'll miss the turn."

Caveman slammed on his brakes in time to pull into the parking lot.

Grace braced her hands on the backs of the seats and swayed with the vehicle as it made the sharp turn. "I was okay, until you nearly gave me whiplash." She didn't wait for him to come to a complete stop before she pushed open her door and dropped down from the truck, crumpling to the ground.

Out of the truck and around the front, Caveman bent to help, sliding his hands beneath her thighs. "We're going to the clinic."

She pushed him away. "I don't need to be carried. I can stand on my own."

"As you have so clearly demonstrated." He drew in a breath and let it out slowly. "Fine. At least let me help you stand upright." He slipped an arm around her waist and lifted her to her feet.

When she was standing on her own, she nodded. "I've got it now."

"Uh-huh. Prove it." He let go of her for a brief moment.

Grace swayed and would have fallen if he'd let her. But he didn't. Instead he wrapped his arm around her waist again and led her into the sheriff's office.

With his help, she made it inside to the front desk.

The deputy on the other side glanced up with a slight frown, his gaze on Caveman. "May I help you?" His frown deepened as he looked toward the woman leaning on Caveman. "Grace?" He popped up from his desk. "Are you all right?"

"I'm fine, Johnny. Is Sheriff Scott in? I need to talk to him ASAP."

"Yeah. I'll get him." He glanced from her to Caveman and back. "As long as you're okay."

Anger simmered beneath the surface. Caveman glanced at the man's name tag. "Deputy Pierce, just get the damn sheriff. I'm not going to hurt her. If I was, I would have left her lying where her horse threw her."

The deputy's lips twitched. "Going." He spun on his heels and hurried through a door and down a hallway. A moment later, he returned with an older man, dressed in a similar tan shirt and brown slacks. "Grace, Johnny said you were thrown by your horse." He held out his hand. "Shouldn't you be at the clinic?"

Grace took the proffered hand and shook her head. "I don't need to see a doctor. I need you and your men to follow me back out to the trail I was on. Now."

"Why? What's wrong?" Sheriff Scott squeezed her hand between both of his. "The wolves in trouble?"

"It's not the wolves I'm worried about right now." She drew in a deep breath. "There was a man. Actually there were two men." She stiffened in the curve of Caveman's arm. "Hell, Sheriff, I witnessed a murder." She let her hand drop to her side as she sagged against Caveman. "I saw it all happen...and I was too far away...to do anything to stop it." She sniffed. "You have to get out there. Just in case he isn't dead. It'll get dark soon. The wolves will find him."

"Is that why you were riding your horse like you were?" Caveman asked.

She nodded. "That, and someone was shooting at me. That's why Bear threw me." Her head came up and she stared at the sheriff. "I need to find Bear. He's running around out there, probably scared out of his mind."

Sheriff Scott touched her arm. "I'll send someone out to look for him and bring him back to your place." He glanced at Caveman. "And you are?"

"Max Decker. But my friends call me Caveman."

The sheriff's eyes narrowed. "And what do you have to do with all of this?"

Grace leaned back and stared up at the man she'd been leaning on. "Yeah, why were you out in the middle of nowhere?"

"I was sent to check on a Mr. Khalig, a pipeline inspector for Rocky Mountain Pipeline Inc. I was told he'd been receiving threats."

"RJ Khalig?" the sheriff asked.

Caveman nodded. "That's the one."

"He's been a regular at the Blue Moose Tavern since he arrived in town a couple weeks ago. He's staying at Mama Jo's Bed-and-Breakfast," Sheriff Scott added.

Grace shook her head. "I'll bet he's the man I saw get shot. He appeared to be checking some device in a valley when the shooter took him down."

"What exactly did you see?" Sheriff Scott asked.

"Yeah," Caveman said. "I'd like to know, as well."

GRACE'S INSIDES CLENCHED and her pulse sped up. "I was searching for one of the wolves we'd collared last spring. His transponder still works, but hasn't moved in the past two days. Either he's lost his collar, or he's dead. I needed to know." Grace took a breath and let it out, the horror of the scene she'd witnessed threatening to overwhelm her.

"I was coming up to the top of a hill, hoping to see the wolf pack in the valley below, so I tied my horse to a tree short of the crown of the ridge. When I climbed to the crest, I saw a vehicle on a hilltop on the other side of the valley. It was an all-terrain vehicle, a four-wheeler. I thought maybe the rider had fallen off or was hurt, so I looked for him and spotted him in the shade of a tree, lying in the prone position on the ground, and he was aiming a rifle at something in the valley." She twisted her fingers. "My first thought was of the wolves.

But when I glanced down into the valley, the wolf pack wasn't there. A man was squatting near the ground, looking at a handheld device.

"When I realized what was about to happen, I yelled. But not soon enough. The shooter fired his shot at the same time. The man in the valley didn't have a chance." She met the sheriff's gaze. "I couldn't even go check on him because the shooter must have heard my shout. The next thing I knew, he was aiming his rifle at me." She shivered. "I got on my horse and raced to the bottom of the mountain."

"And he followed?"

She nodded. "He shot at me a couple of times. I thought I might have outrun him, but he caught up about the time I reached the truck and trailer Mr. Decker mentioned. He shot at me, hit the truck, my horse threw me and I woke up in the backseat of Mr. Decker's truck." She inhaled deeply and let it all out. "We have to go back to that valley. If there's even a chance Mr. Khalig is alive, he won't be by morning."

"I'll take my men and check it out."

Grace touched his arm. "I'm going with you. It'll take less time for you to find him if I show you the exact location."

"You need to see a doctor," the sheriff said. "As you said, I don't have time to wait for that." He glanced at Caveman. "Do you want me to have one of my deputies take you to the clinic?"

Grace's lips firmed into a straight line. "I'm not going to a clinic. I'm going back to check on that man. I won't rest until I know what happened to him. If you won't take me, I'll get on my own four-wheeler and go up there. You're going to need all-terrain vehicles, anyway. Your truck won't make it up those trails."

The sheriff nodded toward his deputy. "Load up the trailer with the two four-wheelers. We're going into the mountains." He faced Grace. "And we're taking her with us."

"I'll meet you out at Khalig's truck in fifteen minutes. It'll take me that long to get to my place, grab my four-wheeler and get back to the location." She faced Caveman. "Do you mind dropping me off at my house? It's at the end of Main Street."

"I'm going with you," Caveman said.

"You're under no obligation to," she pointed out.

"No, but when you find an unconscious woman in the wilderness, you tend to invest in her well-being." His eyes narrowed. He could be as stubborn as she was. "I'm going."

"Do you have a four-wheeler?"

"No, but I know someone who probably does." Given the mission of Task Force Safe Haven, Kevin Garner had to have the equipment he needed to navigate the rocky hills and trails. If not horses, he had to have four-wheelers.

"I'm not waiting for you," Grace warned.

"You're not leaving without me," he countered.

"Is that a command?" She raised her brows. "I'll have you know, I'll do whatever the hell I please."

Caveman sighed. "It's a suggestion. Face it, if your shooter is still out there, you'll need protection."

"The sheriff and deputy will provide any protection I might need."

"They will be busy processing a crime scene."

"Then, I can take care of myself," Grace said. "I've been going out in these mountains alone for nearly a decade. I don't need a man to follow me, or protect me."

The sheriff laid a hand on her arm. "Grace,

he's right. We'll be busy processing a crime scene. Once you get us there, we won't have time to keep an eye on you."

"I can keep an eye on myself," she said. "I'm the one person most interested in my own well-being."

Caveman pressed a finger to her lips. "You're an independent woman. I get that. But before now, you probably have never had someone shooting at you. I have." He took her hand. "Even in the worst battlefield scenarios, I rely on my battle buddies to have my back. Let me get your back."

For a moment, she stared at his hand holding hers. Then she glanced up into his gaze. "Fine. But if you can't keep up, I'll leave you behind."

He nodded. "Deal."

SHE GAVE THE truck and trailer's location to the sheriff and the deputy. Because she didn't want to slow them down from getting out to the site, she was forced to accept a ride from the man who'd picked her up off the ground and carried her around like she was little more than a child.

A shiver slipped through her at the thought of Caveman touching her body in places that hadn't been touched by a man in too long. And he'd found her unconscious. Had she been in the city, anything could have happened to her. In the mountains, with a shooter after her, she hated to think what would have happened had Caveman not come along when he had.

If the killer hadn't finished her off, the wolves, a bear, a mountain lion could have done it for him. Much as she hated to admit it, she was glad the stranger had come along and tucked her into the backseat of his truck.

"We'll meet you in fifteen minutes," Grace said to the sheriff.

He tipped his cowboy hat. "Roger." Then he was all business back on the telephone before Grace made it to the door.

Once outside, Grace strode toward Caveman's truck, now fully in control of the muscles in her legs. She didn't need to lean on anyone. Nor did she need help getting up into the truck.

Caveman beat her to the truck and opened the passenger door.

She frowned at the gesture, seeing it as a challenge to her ability to take care of herself.

"Just so you don't think I'm being chauvinistic, I always open doors for women. My mother drilled that into my head at a very young age. It's a hard habit to break, and I have no intention of doing that now. It's just being polite."

Grace slid into the seat and gave a low-key grunt. "You don't have to make a big deal out of it," she said through clenched teeth.

Caveman rounded the front of the truck, his broad shoulders and trim waist evidence of a man who took pride in fitness. She'd bet there wasn't an ounce of fat on his body, yet he didn't strut to show off his physique. The man had purpose in his stride, and it wasn't the purpose of looking good, though he'd accomplished that in spades. And he was polite, which made Grace feel churlish and unappreciative of all he'd done for her.

When he slid into the driver's seat beside her, she stared straight ahead, her lips twisting into a wry smile. "Thank you for helping me when I was unconscious. And thank you for giving me a ride to my house." She glanced across at him. "And thank you for opening my door for me. It's nice to know chivalry isn't dead."

His lips twitched. "You're welcome." Twisting the key in the ignition, he shot a glance toward her. "Where to?"

She gave him the directions to her little cottage sitting on an acre of land on the edge of town. She hoped Bear had found his way home after his earlier scare. The town of Grizzly Pass was situated in a valley between hills that led up into the mountains. Grace had ridden out that morning from the little barn behind her house.

As she neared the white clapboard cottage with the wide front porch and antique blue shutters, she leaned forward, trying to see around the house to the barn. Was that a tail swishing near the back gate?

Caveman pulled into the driveway.

Before he could shift into Park, she was out of the truck and hurrying around to the back of the house.

Her protector switched off the engine and hurried after her. "Hey, wait up," he called out.

Grace ignored him, bent and slipped through the fence rails and ran toward the back gate next to the barn, her heart soaring.

Bear stood at the gate, tossing his head and dancing back on his hooves.

She opened the gate and held it wide.

Bear slipped through and turned to nuzzle her hand.

Grace reached into her jeans pocket and

pulled out the piece of carrot she'd planned on giving Bear as a treat at the end of the day. She held it out in the palm of her hand.

Bear's big, velvety lips took the carrot and he crunched it between his teeth, nodding his head in approval.

Wrapping her arms around his neck, Grace hugged the horse, relieved he wasn't hurt by the bullet or by wandering around the countryside and crossing highways. "Hey, big boy. Glad you made it home without me." She held on to his bridle and leaned her forehead against his. "I bet you're hungry and thirsty."

Bear tossed his head and whinnied.

With a laugh, Grace straightened and walked toward the barn. Bear followed.

Inside, she opened the stall door. Bear trotted in.

She removed Bear's bridle and was surprised to find Caveman beside her loosening the leather strap holding the girth around the horse's middle. "I can take care of that," she assured him.

"I know my way around horses," he said, and pulled the saddle from Bear's back. "Tack room?"

"At the back of the barn. I can handle the

rest. I just want to get him situated before we leave."

"No problem." He took the saddle and carried it to the tack room. Caveman reappeared outside the stall. "I'll be right back."

"I'm leaving as soon as I'm done here."

"Understood." He took off at a jog out of the barn.

With her self-appointed protector gone, Grace suddenly had a feeling of being exposed. Shrugging off the insecurity, she went to work, giving the horse food and water, and then closed the stall.

From another stall, she rolled her four-wheeler out into the open. She hadn't ridden it in a month and the last time she had, it had been slow to start. She'd had to charge the battery and probably needed to buy a new one, but she didn't have time now. She'd promised to meet the sheriff in fifteen minutes. Already five had passed.

The next five minutes, she did everything she knew to start the vehicle and it refused.

Just when she was about to give up and call the sheriff, a small engine's roar sounded outside the barn.

She walked out and shook her head.

Caveman sat on a newer-model ATV. "Ready?"

"Where did you get that?"

"My boss dropped it off." He checked the instruments, revved the throttle and looked up. "I thought you'd be gone by now."

"I can't get mine to start, and we're supposed to be there in five minutes."

"Let me take a look." He killed the engine and entered the barn.

Okay, so she wasn't that knowledgeable about mechanics. She knew Wally, who had a small-engine repair shop in his barn. He fixed anything she had issues with. That didn't mean she couldn't take care of herself.

"Your battery is dead." Caveman glanced around. "You got another handy?"

She shook her head. "No. Fresh out."

"Got a helmet?"

She nodded. "Yeah, but I won't need it if I can't get my ATV started."

He spun and headed for the barn door. "You can ride on the back of mine," he called out over his shoulder.

Grace's heart fluttered at the thought riding behind Caveman, holding him around the waist to keep from falling off. "No, thanks. Those trails are dangerous." She suspected the danger was more in how her pulse quickened around the man than the possibility of plunging over the edge of a drop-off.

"I grew up riding horses and four-wheelers on rugged mountain trails. I won't let you fall off a cliff." He held up a hand. "Promise."

She frowned. But she knew she only had a few minutes to get to the meeting location and relented, sighing. "Okay. I guess I'll put my life in your hands." She followed him out of the barn and closed the door behind her. "Although I don't know why I should trust you. I don't even know you."

Chapter Three

Caveman settled on the seat of the ATV and tipped his head toward the rear. "Hop on."

Grace fitted her helmet on her head and buckled the strap beneath her chin. "Wouldn't it make more sense for me to drive, since I know the way?"

"Actually, it does." He grinned, scooted to the back of the seat and glanced toward her, raising his brows in challenge.

Still, Grace hesitated for a moment, gnawing on her bottom lip.

God, when she did that, Caveman's groin clenched and he fought the urge to kiss that worried lip and suck it into his mouth. The woman probably had no clue how crazy she could make a man. And he was no exception.

Finally, she slid onto the seat in front of

Caveman. "Hold on." She thumbed the throttle and the four-wheeler leaped forward.

Caveman wrapped his arms around her waist and pressed his chest to her back. Oh, yeah, this was much better than driving.

Grace aimed for the back gate to the pasture, blew through and followed a dirt road up into the hills, zigzagging through fields and gullies until she crossed a highway and ended up on the road leading to Khalig's truck and trailer. Another truck and trailer stood beside the original, this one marked with the county sheriff logo. Sheriff Scott and Deputy Pierce were mounted on four-wheelers.

Grace nodded as she passed them, leading the way up the side of a mountain, the trail narrowing significantly. There was no way a full-size truck or even an SUV could navigate the trajectories. Barely wide enough for the four-wheeler, the path clung to the side of a bluff. The downhill side was so steep it might as well be considered a drop-off. Anyone who fell over the edge wouldn't stop until they hit the bottom a hundred or more feet below.

Now not so sure he'd chosen the right position, Caveman wished he had control of steering the ATV. He tightened his arms around

Grace's slim waist, wondering if she had the strength to keep them both on the vehicle if they hit a really big bump.

Caveman vowed to be the driver on the way back down the mountain. In the meantime, he concentrated on leaning into the curves and staying on the ATV.

As they neared the top of a steep hill, Grace slowed and rolled to a stop. "This is where I tied off my horse."

The sheriff and deputy pulled up beside them. Everyone dismounted.

Fighting the urge to drop to a prone position on the ground and kiss the earth, Caveman stood and pretended the ride up the treacherous trail hadn't been a big deal at all. "You rode your horse down that trail?"

She nodded. "Normally, I take it slowly. But I had a gunman taking shots at me. I let Bear have his head. I have to admit, I wanted to close my eyes several times on the way down."

The sheriff nodded toward the ridgeline. "Was that your vantage point?"

She nodded, but didn't move toward the top. "The shooter was on the ridge to the north."

Sheriff Scott and the deputy drew their weapons and climbed. As they neared the top, they dropped to their bellies and low-crawled the rest of the way. The sheriff lifted binoculars to his eyes.

Caveman stayed with Grace in case the shooter was watching for her.

A couple minutes later, Sheriff Scott waved. "All clear. Grace, I need you to show me what you were talking about."

Grace frowned, scrambled up to the top and squatted beside the sheriff.

Caveman followed, his gaze taking in the valley below and the ridge to the north. Nothing moved and nothing stood out as not belonging.

Grace pointed to the opposite hilltop. "The shooter was over there." Then she glanced down at the valley, her frown deepening. "The man he shot was in the valley just to the right of that pine."

The sheriff raised his binoculars to his eyes again. "He's not there."

"What?" She held out her hand. "Let me see."

Sheriff Scott handed her the binoculars. Grace adjusted them and stared down at the valley below. "I don't understand. He was in that valley. Hell, his truck and trailer are still parked back at the road. Where could he have gone?" She handed the binoculars back to the sheriff. "Do you think he was only wounded and crawled beneath a bush or something?" She was on her feet and headed back to the ATV. "We need to get down there. If that man is still alive, he could be in a bad way."

The sheriff hurried to catch up to her. "Grace, I want you to stay up here with Mr. Decker."

She'd reached the ATV and had thrown her leg over the seat before she turned to stare at the sheriff. "Are you kidding? I left him once, when I could have saved him."

The sheriff shook his head. "You don't know that. You could have ended up a second victim, and nobody would have known where to find either one of you." He touched her arm. "You did the right thing by coming straight to my office."

When the lawman turned away, Grace captured his hand. "Sheriff, I need to know. I feel like I could have done something to stop that man from shooting the other guy. I know it's irrational, but somehow I feel responsible."

The way she stared at the sheriff with her

soft gray eyes made Caveman want the sheriff to let her accompany him to the valley floor.

"You promise to stay back enough not to disturb what could potentially be a crime scene?" Sheriff Scott asked.

She held up her hand like she was swearing in front of a judge. "I promise."

The sheriff shot a glance at Caveman. "Mr. Decker, will you keep an eye on her to make sure she's safe?"

"I will," Caveman said. He wanted to know what was in that valley as well, but if it meant leaving Grace alone on the ridge, he would have stayed with her.

"Fine. Come along, but stay back." Sheriff Scott and the deputy climbed onto their four-wheelers and eased their way down a narrow path to the valley floor.

Caveman let Grace drive again, knowing she was better protected with his body wrapped around her than if she'd ridden on the back.

At the bottom of the hill, Grace parked the four-wheeler twenty yards from the pine tree she'd indicated. "We'll see a lot more on foot than on an ATV."

"True." Caveman studied the surrounding

area, careful to stay out of the way of the sheriff and his deputy.

"Grace," the sheriff called out.

She and Caveman hurried over to where the sheriff squatted on his haunches, staring at the dirt. He pointed. "Is this the spot where he fell?"

Grace glanced around at the nearby tree and nodded. "I think so."

The sheriff's lips pressed together and he pointed at the ground. "This looks like dried blood."

Caveman stared at the dark blotches, his belly tightening. He'd seen similar dark stains in the dust of an Afghanistan village where his brothers in arms had bled out.

"Got tire tracks here." Deputy Pierce stared at the ground a few yards away.

The sheriff straightened and walked slowly toward the deputy. "And there's a trail of blood leading toward the tracks."

Caveman circled wide, studying the ground until he saw what he thought he might find. "More tracks over here." The tracks led toward a hill. Without waiting for permission, Caveman climbed the hill, parallel to the tracks. As the ground grew rockier, the tracks became harder to follow. At that point, Caveman looked for disturbed pebbles, scraped rocks and anything that would indicate a heavy four-wheeler had passed that direction.

At the top of the hill, the slope leveled off briefly and then fell in a sheer two-hundred-foot drop-off to a boulder-strewn creek bed below. Caveman's stomach tightened as he spotted what appeared to be the wreckage of an ATV. "I found the ATV." He squinted. What was that next to the big boulder shaped like an anvil? He leaned over the edge a little farther and noticed what appeared to be a shoe…attached to a foot. "I'm sorry to say, but I think I found Mr. Khalig."

Grace scrambled to the top of the hill and nearly pitched over the edge.

Caveman shot out his hand, stopping her short of following the pipeline inspector to a horrible death. "Oh, dear Lord."

Wrapping his arm around her shoulders, Caveman pulled her against him.

She burrowed her face into his chest. "I should have stayed."

"You couldn't," Caveman said. "You would have been shot."

"I could have circled back," she said, her voice quivering.

"On that trail?" Caveman shook his head. "No way. You did the right thing."

Sheriff Scott appeared beside Caveman. "Mr. Decker's right. You wouldn't be alive if you'd stopped to help a man who could have been dead before he went over the edge."

Grace lifted her head and stared at the sheriff through watery eyes. "What do you mean?"

"We noticed footprints and drag marks in the dirt back there," Deputy Pierce said.

The sheriff nodded. "I suspect the killer came back, dragged the body onto the ATV and rode it up to the hill. Then he pushed it over the edge with Mr. Khalig still on it." He glanced over at the deputy. "We'll get the state rescue team in to recover the body. The coroner will conduct an autopsy. He'll know whether the bullet killed him or the fall."

"Is there anything we can do to help?" Grace asked.

Sheriff Scott nodded. "I'd like you to come in and sign a statement detailing what you saw and at what time."

"Anything you need. I'll be there." Grace shivered. "I wish I'd seen the killer's face."

"I do, too." The sheriff stared down at the creek bed. "Murder cases are seldom solved so easily." He glanced across at Grace. "You might want to watch your back. If he thinks you could pick him out in a lineup, he might come after you."

Grace shivered again. "We live in a small town." Her gaze captured the sheriff's. "There's a good chance I might know him."

"If the law isn't knocking on his door within twenty-four hours," Caveman said, "he might figure out that you didn't see enough of him to turn him in."

"In which case, he'd be smart to keep a low profile and leave you alone," the sheriff added.

"Or not." Grace sighed. "I can't stay holed up in my house. I have work to do. I still haven't found my wolf."

"It might not be safe for you to be roaming the woods right now," the sheriff said. "By yourself, you present an easy target with no witnesses."

Grace's shoulders squared. "I won't let fear run my life. I ran today, and Mr. Khalig is dead because I did."

Caveman shook his head. "No, Mr. Khalig is dead because someone shot him. Not because you didn't stop that someone from shooting him. You are not responsible for that man's death. You didn't pull the trigger." The words were an echo from his psychologist's arsenal of phrases she'd used to help him through survivor's guilt. Using them now with Grace helped him see the truth of them.

He hadn't detonated the bomb that had killed his teammates, nor had he pulled the trigger on the AK-47s that had taken out more of his battle buddies. He couldn't have done anything differently other than die in his teammates' place by being the forward element at that exact moment. He couldn't have known. It didn't make it easier. Only time would help him accept the truth.

"THERE IS SOMETHING you could do for me," the sheriff said.

Grace perked up. "Anything." After all that had happened, she refused to be a victim. She wanted to help.

"Go back down, get in my service vehicle and let dispatch know to call in the mountain rescue crew. Johnny and I will stay and make sure the wolves don't clean up before they get here."

"Will do," Grace said. "Do you need me to come back?"

"No. We can handle it from here. You should head home. And please consider lying low for a while until we're sure the killer isn't still gunning for you."

"Okay," Grace said. Though she had work to do, she now knew she wasn't keen on being the target of a gunman. She'd give it at least a day for the man to realize she hadn't seen him and couldn't identify his face. "You'll let me know what they find out about the man down there?"

"You bet," Sherriff Scott said. "Thank you, Grace, for letting us know as soon as possible."

But not soon enough to help Mr. Khalig. She turned and started back down the hill. Her feet slipped in the gravel and she would have fallen, but Caveman was right beside her and helped her get steady on her feet. He hooked her elbow and assisted her the rest of the way down the steep incline.

At the bottom, he turned her to face him. "Are you okay?"

She nodded. "I'm fine, just a little shaken. It's not every day I witness a murder."

His lips twisted. "How many murders have you witnessed?"

"Counting today?" She snorted. "One." With a nod toward the ATV, she said, "You can drive. I'm not sure I can hold it steady." She held up a hand, demonstrating how much it trembled.

"Thanks. I would rather navigate the downhill trail. Coming up was bad enough." He climbed onto the ATV and scooted forward, allowing room for her to mount behind him.

At this point, Grace didn't care that he was a stranger. The man had found her unconscious, sought help for her and then gone with her to show the sheriff where a murder had taken place. If he'd been the shooter, he'd have killed her by now and avoided the sheriff altogether.

She slipped onto the seat and held on to the metal rack bolted to the back of the machine, thinking it would be enough to keep her seated.

"You need to hold on around my waist," Caveman advised. "It's a lot different being on the back than holding on to the handlebars."

"I'll be okay," she assured him.

Caveman shrugged, started the engine and eased his thumb onto the throttle.

The ATV leapt forward, nearly leaving Grace behind.

She swallowed a yelp, wrapped her arms

around his waist and didn't argue anymore as they traversed the downhill trail to the bottom.

When she'd been the target of the shooter, she hadn't had time to worry about falling off her sure-footed horse. Now that she wasn't in control of the ATV and was completely reliant on Caveman, she felt every bump and worried the next would be the one that would throw her over the edge. She tightened her hold around his middle, slightly reassured by the solid muscles beneath his shirt.

For a moment, she closed her eyes and inhaled the scent of pure male—a mix of aftershave and raw, outdoor sensuality. It calmed her.

Although she'd always valued her independence, she could appreciate having someone to lean on in this new and dangerous world she lived in. Before, she'd only had to worry about bears and wolves killing her. Now she had to worry about a man diabolical enough to hunt another man down like an animal.

By the time they finally reached the bottom and made their way back to the parked trucks, Grace's body had adjusted to Caveman's movements, making them seem like one person—

riding the trails, absorbing every bump and leaning into every turn.

When the vehicles came into view, she pulled herself back to the task at hand.

Caveman stopped next to the sheriff's truck and switched off the ATV's engine.

Grace climbed off the back, the cool mountain air hitting her front where the heat generated by Caveman still clung to her. Shaking off the feeling of loss, she opened the passenger door of the sheriff's vehicle, slid onto the front seat, grabbed the radio mic and pressed the button. "Hello."

"This is dispatch, who am I talking to?"

"Grace Saunders. Sheriff Scott wanted me to relay a request for a mountain rescue team to be deployed to his location as soon as possible."

"Could you provide a little detail to pass on to the team?" the dispatcher asked.

Grace inhaled and let out a long slow breath before responding. "There's a man at the bottom of a deep drop-off."

"Is he unconscious?"

The hollow feeling in her chest intensified. "We believe he's dead. He's not moving and he could be the victim of a gunshot wound."

"Got it. I'll relay the GPS coordinate and have the team sent out as soon as they can mobilize."

"Thank you." Grace hung the mic on the radio and climbed out of the sheriff's SUV.

"Now what?" Caveman asked. He'd dismounted from the four-wheeler and stepped up beside the sheriff's vehicle while she'd been talking on the radio.

She shrugged. "If you could take me back to my place, I have work to do."

Caveman frowned. "When we get there, will you let me take you to the clinic to see a doctor?"

"I don't need one." Her head hurt and she was a little nauseated, but she wouldn't admit it to him. "I'd rather stay home."

"I'll make a deal with you. I'll take you home if you promise to let me take you from there to see a doctor."

She sighed. "You're not going to let it go, are you?"

He crossed his arms over his chest and shook his head. "Nope."

"And if I don't agree, either I walk home— which I don't mind, but I'm not in the mood—

or I wait until the sheriff is done retrieving Mr. Khalig's body."

His lips twitched. "That about sums it up. See a doctor, walk home alone or wait for a very long time." He raised his hands, palms up. "It's a no-brainer to me."

Her eyes narrowed. "I'll walk." She brushed past him and lengthened her stride, knowing she was too emotionally exhausted to make the long trek all the way back to her house, but too stubborn to let Caveman win the argument.

The ATV roared to life behind her and the crunch of gravel heralded its approach.

"You might also consider that by walking home, you put yourself up as an easy target for a man who has proven he can take a man down from a significant distance. Are you willing to be his next target?"

His words socked her in the gut. She stopped in her tracks and her lips pressed together in a hard line.

Damn. The man had a good point. "Fine." She spun and slipped her leg over the back of the four-wheeler. "You can take me to my house. From there, I'll take myself to the clinic."

Caveman shook his head, refusing to engage

the engine and send the ATV toward Grace's house. "That's not the deal. I take you home. Then I will take you to the clinic. When the doctor clears you to drive, you can take yourself anywhere you want to go."

"Okay. We'll do it your way." She wrapped her arms loosely around his waist, unwilling to be caught up in the pheromones the man put off. "Can we go, already?"

"Now we can go." He goosed the throttle. The ATV jumped, nearly unseating Grace.

She tightened her hold around Caveman's waist and pressed her body against his as they bumped along the dirt road with more potholes than she remembered on the way out. Perhaps because she noticed them more this time because she wasn't the one in control of the steering. Either way, she held on, her thighs tightly clamped around his hips and the seat.

By the time they arrived at her cottage, she could barely breathe—the fact having nothing to do with the actual ride so much as it did with the feel of the man's body pressed against hers. She was almost disappointed when he brought the vehicle to a standstill next to her gate.

Grace climbed off and opened the gate. The distance between them helped her to get her head on straight and for her pulse to slow down to normal.

He followed her to her house. "We'll take my truck. Grab your purse and whatever else you'll need."

When she opened her mouth to protest, he held up his hand.

"You promised." He frowned and crossed his arms over his chest again. "Where I come from, a promise is sacred."

Her brows met in the middle. "Where *do* you come from?"

His frown disappeared and he grinned. "Montana."

Caveman started toward the house, Grace fell in step beside him. "Is that where you were before you arrived in Grizzly Pass?"

His grin slipped. "No."

She shot a glance his direction. A shadow had descended on his face and he appeared to be ten years older.

"Where *did* you come from?"

He stared out at the mountains. "Bethesda, Maryland."

There was so much she didn't know about this man. "That's a long way from Montana."

"Yes, it is." He stopped short of her porch.

"I'll be in my truck when you're ready." Before she could say more, he turned and strode toward the corner of her house.

For a moment, Grace allowed herself the pleasure of watching the way his butt twitched in his blue jeans. The man was pure male and so ruggedly handsome he took her breath away. What was he doing hanging around her? Since she was being forced to ride with him to the clinic, she'd drill him with questions until she was satisfied with the answers. For starters, why did he call himself Caveman? And what was the importance of Bethesda, Maryland, that had made him go from being relaxed and helpful to stiff and unapproachable?

Caveman disappeared around the corner.

Grace faced her house, fished her key from her pocket and climbed the stairs. She opened the screen door and held out the key, ready to fit it into the lock when she noticed something hanging on the handle. It rocked back and forth and then fell at her feet.

She jumped back, emitting a short, sharp scream, her heart thundering against her ribs. With her hand pressed to her chest, she squatted and stared at the item, a lead weight settling in the pit of her belly as she recognized the circular band with the rectangular plastic box affixed to it.

It was the radio collar for the wolf she'd been looking for earlier that day, and it was covered in blood.

Chapter Four

Caveman had been about to climb into his truck when he heard Grace's scream. All thoughts of Bethesda, physical therapy and war wounds disappeared in a split second. He pulled his pistol from beneath the seat and raced back around the house to find Grace sitting on the porch, her back leaning against the screen door, her hand pressed to her chest.

"What's wrong?" His heart thundered against his ribs and his breathing was erratic as he stared around the back porch, searching for the threat.

"This." She pointed toward something on the porch in front of her. It appeared to be some kind of collar. Her gaze rose to his, her eyes wide, filling with tears. "This is the collar for the wolf I was looking for when I ran across the murder scene."

"What the hell's it doing here?"

"It was hanging on the handle of the door. Someone put it there."

"Do you have any coworkers who would have brought it to you?" Caveman reached out a hand to her.

She laid her slim fingers into his palm and allowed him to pull her to her feet and into his arms. "It has blood on it and it's been cut."

"Why would someone put it on your doorknob?" he asked.

She drew in a deep breath and let it out. "I was out in the mountains where I was because I was following the signal for this collar. It had stopped moving as of two days ago. The only other people aware of the wolf's movement, or lack thereof, were my coworkers on the Wolf Project out of Yellowstone National Park. This collar belonged to Loki, a black male wolf out of Molly's pack. I rescued him as a cub when his mother had been killed by a local rancher." Her jaw tightened, she drew herself up and gave him a level stare through moist eyes. "We suspected he was dead, but had hoped of natural causes. That someone brought me the collar without a note of why it was covered in blood leaves me to think all kinds of bad things."

"You think the shooter who killed Khalig might have killed the wolf?"

"If he didn't kill the wolf, I think he wants me to believe he did."

"And he left the collar as a warning or a trophy?"

Grace stared down at the offensive object and nodded. "What else am I supposed to think? Unless someone else owns up to leaving the collar on my back porch doorknob, I can only imagine why it was left." She bent, reaching for the collar.

Caveman grabbed her arm to keep her from retrieving it. "Leave it there for the sheriff. They might be able to pull fingerprints from the plastic box."

Grace straightened. "Why do people have to be so destructive and heartless with nature?"

"I don't know, but let's get you inside, just in case the shooter is lurking nearby."

Grace shot a glance over her shoulder. "Do you think he might be out there watching?" A shiver shook her body.

"He could be." Caveman held out his hand. "Let me have your key."

She pointed at the porch near the collar. "I dropped it."

Caveman retrieved it from the porch and straightened. "Let's go through the front door." Slipping his arm around her, he shielded her body with his as much as possible as he led her around the house to the front door. There he opened the screen door. Before he fit the key into the lock, he tried the knob. It was locked. He fit the key in the knob, twisted and pushed the door open. "Let me go first."

She nodded and allowed him to enter first, following right behind him.

Closing the door behind her, he stared down into her eyes. "I want to check the house. Stay here."

Again, she nodded.

Caveman moved from room to room, holding his 9-millimeter pistol in front of him, checking around the corners of each wall before moving into a room. When he reached the back door, he checked the handle. The door was locked. As far as he could tell, the house hadn't been entered. "All clear," he called out.

"The sheriff will be busy up in the hills until

they retrieve the body," Grace said, walking into the kitchen, her arms wrapped around her body. "I don't like the idea of leaving the collar on the porch."

"Do you have a paper bag we can use and maybe some rubber gloves?"

"I do." She hurried into a pantry off the kitchen and emerged with a box of rubber gloves and what appeared to be a paper lunch bag. Setting the box of gloves on the counter, she pulled on a pair. "These won't fit your big hands. I'll take care of the collar."

He opened the back door and looked before stepping over the collar and standing on the porch. He used his body as a shield to protect Grace in case the shooter had her in his sights. Given the killer had good aim with a rifle and scope, he could be hiding in the nearby woods, his sights trained on her back door.

Grace scooped up the collar by the nylon band and dropped it into the paper bag, touching as little as possible.

Once she had the collar in the bag, she nodded. "I'll grab my purse. We can drop this off at the sheriff's office."

"On the way to the clinic," Caveman added.

Her lush lips pulled into a twisted frown.

"On the way to the clinic." The frown turned up on the corners. "You are a stubborn man, aren't you?"

He grinned and followed her back into the house, locking the door behind him. "I prefer to call it being persistent."

She walked back through the house. "If you give me just a minute, I'd like to wash my hands and face."

"Take your time. I'll wait by the front door."

Grace turned down the hallway and ducked into the bathroom, closing the door behind her.

Caveman waited in the front entrance, staring at the pictures hanging on the walls. Many were of wolves. Some were of people. One had a group of men and women standing in front of a cabin, all grinning, wearing outdoor clothing. Another photo was of Grace, maybe a few years younger, with a man. They were kissing with the sun setting over snowcapped peaks in the background. She looked young, happy and in love.

Something tugged at Caveman's chest. He'd assumed Grace was single.

The door opened to the bathroom and Grace appeared, her face freshly scrubbed, still makeup-free. She'd brushed her hair and left it falling around her shoulders the way it was in the picture.

"You have some interesting pictures on your wall." Caveman nodded toward the wolves.

She nodded. "I'm living my dream job as a biologist working on the Wolf Project, among others. The pictures are of some of the wolves I've been tracking for the past five years."

Caveman pointed toward the group picture.

Grace smiled. "Those are the crew of biologists working in Yellowstone National Park. We keep in touch by phone, internet and through in-person meetings once a month."

"Do you live alone?" Caveman asked, his gaze on the picture of her kissing the man. "Should I be concerned about a jealous husband walking through the door at any moment?"

The smile left Grace's eyes. "Yes, I live alone. No, you don't have to worry." She grabbed a brown leather purse from a hallway table and opened the front door. "I'm ready."

"I take it I hit a sore spot," he said, passing her to exit the house first.

"I'm not married, anymore."

But she was once. Caveman vowed not to pry. Apparently, she wasn't over her ex-husband. Not if she still had his picture hanging in her front entrance.

Grace paused to lock the front door and then turned to follow him toward the truck. "For the record, I'm a widow. My husband died in a parasailing accident six years ago."

GRACE CLIMBED INTO the passenger seat of Caveman's truck. "You really don't have to take me to the clinic. I've been getting around fine for the past couple of hours without blacking out. I could drive myself there, for that matter."

"Humor me. I feel—"

"Responsible," she finished for him. "Well, you're not. You've done more than you had to. You could have dropped me off at the sheriff's office earlier today and been done with me."

"That's not the kind of guy I am."

She tilted her head and stared across the console at him. "No, I got that impression." She settled back in her seat, closed her eyes and let him take control, something she wasn't quite used to. "Well, thank you for coming to my rescue. If you hadn't been there…" She shivered. What would have happened? Would the shooter have caught up to her and finished her off like he'd done Mr. Khalig?

A hand touched hers.

She opened her eyes, her gaze going to where his hand held hers and warmth spread from that point throughout her body. She hadn't had that kind of reaction to a man's touch since Jack had died, and she wasn't sure she wanted it.

"I'm glad I was there." Caveman squeezed her fingers gently, briefly and let go. "I'm sorry about your husband."

"Yeah. Me, too. We were supposed to be doing this together." She shrugged and let go of the breath she hadn't known she was holding the whole time Caveman's hand had been on hers. "But that was six years ago. Life goes on. Turn left at the next street. The clinic is three blocks on the right."

They arrived in front of the Grizzly Pass Clinic a few minutes before it was due to close. "I doubt they can get me in."

"If they can't, where's the nearest emergency room?" Caveman shifted into Park and stepped down from the truck. Rounding the front of the vehicle, he arrived in time to help her down.

"The nearest would be in Bozeman, an hour and a half away."

"Guess we better get inside quickly." He

cupped her elbow and guided her through the door.

Fortunately, the doctor had enough time left to check her over while her self-appointed bodyguard waited in the lobby.

"You appear to be all right. If you get any dizzy spells or feel nauseated, you might want to call the EMTs and have them transport you to the nearest hospital for further evaluation. But so far, I don't see anything that makes me too concerned." He offered her a prescription for painkillers, which she refused. "Then take some over-the-counter pain relievers if you get a headache."

She smiled. "Thank you for seeing me on such short notice."

"I'm glad I was here for you." He walked her to the door. "Have you considered wearing a helmet when you go horseback riding?"

"I have considered it. And I might resort to it, if I continue to fall off my horse." She might also consider a bulletproof vest and making the helmet a bulletproof one if she continued to be the target of a sniper. She didn't say it out loud, nor had she told the doctor why she'd fallen off her horse. The medical professional had been

ready to go home before she'd shown up and
he wasn't the one being shot at.

When she stepped out of the examina-
tion room into the lobby, she found Caveman
laughing at something the cute receptionist had
said. The smile on his face transformed him
from the serious, rugged cowboy to someone
more lighthearted and approachable. The sparkle in his eyes made him even more handsome
than before.

A territorial feeling washed over Grace.
Suddenly she had a better understanding of
the urge the alpha wolf had to guard his mate
and keep her to himself. Not that Caveman was
Grace's mate. Hell, they'd just met!

But that didn't stop her fingers from curling
into her palms or her gut from clenching when
the receptionist smiled up at the man.

"Are you ready to take me home?" Grace
asked, her voice a little sharper than usual.

Caveman straightened and turned his smile
toward her, brightening the entire room with its
full force. Then it faded and his brows pulled
together. "What did the doctor say?"

"I'm fine. Can we go now?" She started for
the door, ready to leave the office and the cute,
young receptionist as soon as possible.

Grace was outside on the sidewalk by the time Caveman caught up with her and gripped her arm. "Slow down. It might not be safe for you to be out in the open. Care to elaborate on the doctor's prognosis?"

"He said I'm fine and can carry on, business as usual." She shook off his hand.

"No concussion?"

"No concussion. Which means you can drop me off at my house, and your responsibility toward me is complete."

He nodded and opened the truck door for her. "If you don't mind, I'd like to stop by my boss's office for a few minutes. I need to brief him on what happened. He might want to hear what you have to say."

"Now that we're not being shot at, and I'm not dying of a concussion, maybe you can answer a few questions for me."

"Shoot." He winced. "Sorry. I didn't mean the pun."

She inhaled and thought of all the questions she had for this man. "Okay. Who's your boss?"

"The US Army, but I'm on temporary loan to a special task force with the Department of

Homeland Security. I'm reporting to a man named Kevin Garner."

"I've seen Kevin around. I didn't know he was heading a special task force."

"It's new. I'm new. I got in a couple days ago, and I'm still trying to figure out what it is I'm supposed to be doing."

"Army?" That would explain the short hair, the military bearing and the scars. "For how long?"

"Eleven years."

"Deployed?"

He nodded, his gaze on the road ahead. "What is this? An interrogation?"

"I've been all over the mountains with you and I don't know who you are."

"I told you, I'm Max Decker, but my friends call me—"

"Caveman." She crossed her arms over her chest. "Why?"

"Why what?"

"Why do they call you Caveman?"

"I don't know. I guess because I look like a caveman? I got tagged with it in Delta Force training, and it's stuck ever since."

"Army Delta Force?" She looked at him anew. "Isn't that like the elite of the elite?"

He shrugged. "I like to think of it as highly skilled. I'm not an elitist."

"And you're assigned to the Department of Homeland Security?" She shook her head. "Who'd you make mad?"

His fingers tightened on the steering wheel until his knuckles turned white. "I'd like to know that myself."

"Wait." Her eyes narrowed. "You said you came from Bethesda. Isn't that where Walter Reed Army Hospital is located?"

A muscle ticked in his jaw. "Yeah. I was injured in battle. I just completed physical therapy and was waiting for orders to return to my unit."

"And you got pulled to help out here." It was a statement, not a question. "Any you carried me to your truck." She raked his body with her gaze. "I don't see you limping or anything."

"I told you. I finished my physical therapy. I've been working out since. I'm back to normal. Well, almost."

"What did you injure?"

He dropped his left hand to his thigh. "My leg."

"Gunshot?"

"Yeah."

"I'm sorry." She dragged her gaze away from him. "I didn't mean to get too personal."

"It's okay. When you're in the hospital, everyone gets pretty damned personal. I'm used to it by now."

"It had to be hard."

"What?"

"The hospital."

His replaced his hand on the steering wheel, as he pulled into the parking lot of the Blue Moose Tavern. "At least I made it to the hospital," he muttered.

Grace heard his words but didn't dig deeper to learn their meaning. She could guess. He'd made it to the hospital. Apparently, some of his teammates hadn't.

Sometimes recovering from an injury was easier than recovering from a loss. She knew. Having lost her husband in a parasailing accident, she understood what it felt like to lose someone you loved.

From what she knew about the Delta Force soldiers, they were a tightly knit organization. A brotherhood. Those guys fought for their country and for each other.

Grace realized she and Caveman had more in common than she'd originally thought.

Chapter Five

Caveman got out of the truck in front of the Blue Moose Tavern, his thoughts on the men who'd lost their lives in that last battle. For a moment, he forgot where he was. He looked up at the sign on the front of the tavern and shook his head.

Like Grace had said, life moves on. He couldn't live in the past. Squaring his shoulders, he focused on the present and the woman who'd witnessed a murder. Kevin would want to hear what she had to say. Since the man who'd been shot was most likely RJ Khalig, it had to have something to do with the threats the man had reported, the reason Garner had sent Caveman out to find the pipeline inspector.

A pang of guilt tugged at his insides. If he

hadn't delayed his departure, arguing over his assigned duties, would he have found Khalig before the sniper?

He shook his head. When he'd arrived at the base of the trail, he wouldn't have been able to find the man without GPS tracking and an all-terrain vehicle. *No.* He couldn't have gotten to Khalig before the shooter.

Grace was out of the truck before Caveman could reach her door. She sniffed the air. "I didn't realize how hungry I was until now."

Caveman inhaled the scent of grilled hamburgers and his mouth watered. "Let's make it quick with Garner. If you're like me, you haven't eaten since breakfast this morning."

"And that was a granola bar." She glanced toward the tavern door. "They make good burgers here."

"Then we'll eat as soon as we're done upstairs." Caveman waved a hand toward the outside staircase leading up to the apartment above the tavern.

Grace rested her hand on the railing and climbed to the top.

Caveman followed closely, once again shielding Grace's body from a sniper's sights.

Before they reached the top landing, the

door swung open. Kevin Garner greeted them. "Caveman, I'm glad you stopped by." He stepped back, allowing them to enter the upstairs apartment. Once they were inside, he closed the door, turned to Grace and held out his hand. "I've seen you in passing, but let me introduce myself. Kevin Garner, Department of Homeland Security."

"Grace Saunders. I'm a biologist assigned to the Wolf Project, working remotely with the National Park Service out of Yellowstone."

"Interesting work." Garner shook her hand. "I'm glad you stopped by. I wanted to hear what happened today. The last thing I knew, you were recovering from being thrown by your horse, and Caveman needed a four-wheeler to go back into the mountains. Care to fill me in on what's happened since you got up this morning?"

Grace spent the next five minutes detailing what she'd seen on that ridge in the mountains and what had followed, taking him all the way to her back porch and the present she'd received.

She held out the paper bag with the dog collar inside. "Can I assume you have some of the same capabilities or access to the same support facilities as the sheriff's office?"

Garner took the bag, opened it and stared inside, his brows furrowing. "What do you have here?"

"The collar for number 755. Loki, the wolf I was tracking when I went up in the mountains this morning."

"I don't understand." His glance shot from Grace to Caveman and back to Grace. "Where's the wolf?"

Her lips firmed into a tight line. "Most likely dead. But I haven't seen the body to confirm." Grace nodded toward the bag. "That was left on my back porch as a gift."

"We suspect that whoever killed Khalig might have killed the wolf and decided to leave this on Grace's back porch," Caveman said.

Kevin's brows twisted. "Why?"

His jaw tightening, Caveman glanced toward Grace. "Possibly as a warning to keep her mouth shut about the murder she witnessed."

Kevin stared at the collar. "Or he might be a sadistic bastard, trying to scare her. Otherwise, why would he kill the wolf?"

"Target practice?" Grace suggested, her face pale, her jaw tight.

"Could he be one of the local ranchers who has lost livestock because of the reintroduction of wolves to the Yellowstone ecosystem?" Garner asked.

Grace nodded. "He could be."

"Or he could be a game hunter wanting a trophy for his collection," Caveman said. "Why else would he remove the collar?"

Grace frowned. "You think he killed the wolf before he took out Mr. Khalig?"

Caveman caught Grace's gaze and held it. "You said, yourself, the collar had been stalled in the same location for two days. He had to have killed the wolf two days ago."

"And he retraced his steps to where he'd killed him just to retrieve the collar?" Grace shook her head. "Doesn't make sense. I saw him kill Mr. Khalig. You'd think he'd get the hell off the mountain and come up with an alibi for where he was when I witnessed the murder."

"Unless he's cocky and wants to play games with you," Caveman said.

Grace shivered and wrapped her arms around her middle. "That's a lot of assumption."

"Still, if this guy thinks he can get away

with the murder, and he's flaunting that fact by gifting you with this collar, you need to be careful," Garner said. "If he thinks you can identify him, he might take it a step further."

Grace turned and paced away from Garner and Caveman. Then she spun and marched back. "I don't have time to play games with a killer. I have work to do."

Caveman closed the distance between them and gripped her arms. "And who will do that work if you're dead?"

She stared up at him, her gray eyes widening. "You really think he'll come after me?"

"He already has once, right after the murder. If he left that collar, that makes two times."

"Three's a charm," Grace muttered, raising her hands to rest on Caveman's chest. Instead of pushing him away, she curled her fingers into his shirt. "What am I supposed to do?"

Garner tapped an ink pen on a tabletop where he had a map of the area spread out. "Khalig had received threats. I hadn't been able to pinpoint from whom. I have to assume whoever was threatening him had to have a gripe with the pipeline industry."

"What kind of threats?" Caveman asked.

"Someone painted 'Go Home' on his company truck's windshield two days ago. Yesterday, he had all four tires slashed. I tried to talk him out of going out into the field until we got to the bottom of it, but he insisted he had work to do."

Caveman raised his brows and stared down at the woman in his arms. "Sound familiar?"

"Okay." Grace rolled her eyes. "I get the point." She stepped back, out of Caveman's grip. "I don't know anything about the pipeline. Except that it goes through this area. Supposedly it's buried deep and not in an active volcanic location."

"There's been quite a bit of controversy about the pipelines and whether or not we should even have them. Activists love a cause," Garner said. "With oil prices going down, a lot of pipeline employees are out of work. That makes for some unhappy people who depended on the pipeline companies for their jobs. Then there are the ranchers who are angry at the pipeline companies having free access to cross their lands."

"And there are the ranchers who are mad at the government interfering with grazing rights on government property," Caveman added. "Like Old Man Vanders, whose herd was confiscated because he refused to pay the required fees for grazing on federally owned land."

Garner nodded. "That's what stirred up a lot of folks around here. There's a local group calling itself Free America. We found empty crates in the Lucky Lou Mine with indication they'd once been full of AR-15 rifles. We think the Free America folks have them and might be preparing to stage an attack on a government facility." Garner raised a hand. "I know. It's a lot to take in. Thus the need for me to borrow some of the best from the military."

Grace shook her head. "I had no idea things were getting so bad around here." She snorted. "With all that, don't forget the ranchers angry with the government for reintroducing wolves to the area. I know I get a lot of nastiness from cattlemen when they find one of their prize heifers downed by a wolf pack."

Caveman crossed his arms over his chest. "Since Khalig is a pipeline inspector, is it safe to assume the shooter targeted him because of something to do with the pipeline?"

"That would be my bet. But that doesn't negate the possibility that Khalig might have stumbled across something secret the Free America militia were plotting."

"He was checking some kind of instrument," Grace reiterated. "From what I could tell, he didn't appear to be afraid or nervous about anything. He straightened, still glancing down at his equipment, when the shooter took him down."

"For whatever reason he was murdered," Garner said, "we don't want anything to happen to you, just because you witnessed it."

Grace stiffened. "Don't worry about me. I can take care of myself."

"Do you own a gun?" Kevin asked.

Her chin tilted upward. "I do. A .40-caliber pistol."

"Do you know how to use it?" Caveman asked.

Her gaze shifted to the wall behind him. "Enough to protect myself."

"Are you sure about that?"

"I know how to load it, to turn off the safety and point it at the target."

"When was the last time you fired the weapon?" Caveman asked.

Her cheeks reddened. "Last year I took it to the range and familiarized with it."

Caveman's eyes widened. "A year?" He

drew in a deep breath and let it out slowly. "Lady, you're no expert."

Her lips firmed and she pushed back her shoulders. "I didn't say I was. I said I knew how to use my gun."

"It's not enough," Garner said.

Grace turned her frown toward the DHS man. "What do you mean?"

Garner's gaze connected with Caveman's.

Caveman's gut tightened. He knew where Garner was going with what he'd just stated, and he knew he was getting the task.

"You need protection," Garner turned toward Grace.

She flung her hands in the air. "Why won't anyone believe me when I say I don't need someone following me around?" Those same hands fisted and planted on her hips. "I can take care of myself. I don't need some stranger intruding in my life."

"I wasn't going to suggest a stranger," Kevin said.

"Well, the sheriff's department has their hands full policing this area and finding a murderer," Grace shook her head. "I wouldn't ask them to babysit me, when I have my own gun."

"You need someone to watch your back."

Garner held up a hand to stop Grace's next flow of words. "I wasn't going to suggest a stranger." He shifted his glance toward Caveman.

His lips twitching on the corners, Caveman couldn't help the grin pulling at his mouth when he stared at the horrified expression on Grace's face. Suddenly, being in Wyoming on temporary duty didn't seem so bad. Not if he could get under the skin of a beautiful biologist. As long as when it was all said and done, he could return to his unit and the career he'd committed his life to.

"YOU WANT *HIM* to follow me around?" Grace waved her hand toward Caveman. "He doesn't even want to be in Wyoming." She narrowed her eyes as she glared at Garner. "And you said you wouldn't suggest a stranger. I didn't know this man until sometime around noon today when I found myself loaded in the backseat of his truck like a kidnap victim." She shook her head. "No offense, but no thanks."

Garner's brows dipped. "Am I missing something? I thought you two were getting along fine."

Oh, they had gotten along fine, but she

couldn't ignore the sensual pull the man had on her. "You are missing something," Grace said. "You're missing the point. I don't need a babysitter. I'm a grown woman, perfectly capable of taking care of myself." Perhaps the more she reiterated the argument, the more she would begin to believe it. Today had shaken her more than she cared to admit.

"Agreed," Garner said. "In most cases. But based on the evidence you've presented, you have a sniper after you. Who better than another sniper to protect you? Caveman is one of the most highly trained soldiers you'll ever have the privilege to meet. He understands how a sniper works, having been one himself."

Grace glanced at Caveman. Was it true? Was he a sniper as well as a trained Delta Force soldier?

He nodded without responding in words.

Her belly tightening, Grace continued to stare at this man who was basically a war hero stuck in Grizzly Pass, Wyoming.

"He's the most qualified person around to make sure you're not the next victim," the Homeland Security man said.

"But I—" Grace started.

"Let me finish." Garner laced his fingers together. "I'll speak with the sheriff's department and ask them if they have someone who could provide twenty-four/seven protection for you."

Grace shook her head. "They don't have the manpower."

"Then I'll query the state police," Garner countered.

"They're stretched thin." Grace wasn't helping herself by shooting down every contingency plan Garner had.

"Look, Grace." Garner lifted her hand. "Let Caveman protect you until I can come up with an alternative." He squeezed her hand. "What's it going to hurt? So you have to put him up for a few nights. You have enough room in your house."

Caveman chuckled. "I promise to clean up after myself. And I can cook—if you like steaks on the grill or carryout."

She chewed on her bottom lip, worry chiseling away at her resistance. "You really think I'm at risk?"

Garner held up the paper bag and nodded. "Yes."

"And you can't always be looking over your shoulder," Caveman added. "I respect your independence, but even the most independent of us need help sometimes. I'll do my best not to disturb your work and stay out of your way as much as I can. The fact is, a killer has taken one life and he's left his calling card on your door. If I was you, I'd want a second pair of eyes watching out for me."

"What do you say?" Garner pressed.

Grace's lips twisted and her eyes narrowed as she stared at Caveman. She didn't want to be around him that much. He stirred up physical responses she hadn't felt since her husband died. It confused her and made her feel off balance. But they were right. She couldn't keep looking over her shoulder. She needed help. "I still want to get out and check on the other wolves."

"We'll talk about it," Caveman said.

"We'll do it," she insisted. "And I won't be confined to my house."

"We'll talk about going out in the woods. And I promise not to confine you to your house." He waved his hand out to the side. "We're having dinner at the tavern today. See? I can be flexible."

Another moment passed and Grace finally conceded. "Okay, but only for the short term. I'm used to living by myself. Having another person in my house will only irritate me."

"Fair enough." Garner grinned. "I'll see what I can do to resolve the situation so that you don't need to have a bodyguard."

"Thank you." Grace's stomach rumbled loudly, her cheeks heated and she gave a weak smile. "As for eating, *clearly* you know that I'm ready."

Again, Caveman chuckled. "Let's feed the beast. We can talk about where to go from here, over a greasy burger and fries."

Her belly growled again at the mention of food. "Now you're talking."

Garner walked them to the door and held it open. "Be careful and stick close to Caveman. He'll protect you."

"What about the collar?" Grace asked.

"I'll get it to the state crime lab. If they can lift prints, they'll be able to run them through the nationwide AFIS database to see if they have a match. I'll let you know as soon as I hear anything."

"Thanks, Kevin." Grace held out her hand.

He took it, his lips lifting on one corner. "You're welcome. I'm glad you'll be with Caveman."

Caveman was first out the door of the up-stairs loft apartment, his gaze scanning the area, searching for anything, or anyone, out of the ordinary or carrying a rifle with a scope. Apparently satisfied the coast was clear, he held out his hand to Grace. "Stay behind me."

"Why behind you?" she asked.

"The best probability of getting a good shot comes from the west." He pointed toward the building on the south. "The buildings provide cover from the north to the south. And I'm your shield from the west. The staircase blocks the shooter's ability to get off a clear shot."

His explanation made sense. "But I don't want you to be a shield. That means if the killer takes a shot, he'll hit you first."

"That's the idea. If that happens, duck as soon as you hear the shot fired. If I'm hit and go down, he'll continue to fire rounds until he gets you."

"Seriously. You can't be that dense." She touched his shoulder, a blast of electricity shooting through her fingers, up her arms and into her chest. "I don't want you to take a bullet for me."

"Most likely the shooter won't be aiming for me. If I'm in the way, he'll wait for me to move out of the way so that he can get to you."

"That makes me feel *so* much better," she

said, her voice strained. "We don't know that he'll come gunning for me, anyway."

"No, we don't. But are you willing to take the risk?"

Grace sighed. "No." What use was it to argue? The longer they were out in the open, the longer Caveman was exposed to Grace's shooter. "Hurry up then, before I pass out from hunger."

A chuckle drifted up to her. "Bossy much?"

"I get cranky when my blood sugar drops."

"I'll try to remember that and bring along snacks to keep that from happening." Caveman paused at the bottom of the stairs, hooked her arm with one of his hands and slipped the other around her shoulders.

Her pulse rocketed and she frowned up at him. "Is that necessary?"

"Absolutely. My arm around you makes it hard for anyone to distinguish one body from the other. Especially at a distance." His lips quirked on the edges. "I'll consider your reaction more of the low blood sugar crankiness."

Again, shut up by a valid argument, Grace suffered in silence. Although suffer was a harsh word when in fact she was far from suffering, unless she considered unfulfilled lust as something to struggle with.

Caveman opened the door to the tavern and waved her inside.

"Grace, it's been a while since you were in." A young woman with bright blond hair and blue eyes greeted them. "Would you like a table or to sit at the bar?"

"Hi, Melissa. We'd like a table," Grace responded.

"Hold on, just a minute. Let me see if there's one available." She disappeared into the crowded room.

"Is it always this busy?" Caveman stared around the room, his brows rising.

"As one of two restaurants in town, yes. The other one doesn't serve alcohol."

"I understand." He glanced around the room. "Do you know most of the people here?"

"Most," she said. "Not all. It's a small town, but we have people drift in who work on the pipeline or cowboys who come in town looking for work."

Caveman nodded. "It was like that in Montana, where I'm from. Everyone knew everyone else."

Melissa appeared in front of them. "I have a

seat ready, if you'll follow me. Is this a date?" she asked, her gaze shooting to Grace.

"No," Grace replied quickly. She wasn't interested in Caveman as anything other than a bodyguard to keep her safe until they caught the killer.

"Oh? Business?" She turned her smile on Caveman.

"You could say that," Grace said.

"Yes, strictly business," Caveman agreed.

"That's nice." Melissa's eyelids dropped low. "In town for long?"

"I don't know," Caveman said.

Grace wasn't sure she liked the smile Melissa gave to Caveman, or that she was openly flirting with him when Grace was on the other side of the man. She wanted to call the girl out on her rude behavior, but was afraid she'd look like a jealous shrew. So she kept her mouth shut and seethed inwardly.

Not that she cared. Caveman could date any woman he wanted. Grace had no hold on him and would never have one. She'd sworn off men years ago, afraid to date one or form a bond. The men she'd been attracted to in the past had all died of one cause or another. The common denominator was their relationship with her.

Though she was a biologist and didn't believe in ghosts or fairy tales, she couldn't refute the evidence. Men who professed an affection for her died. What did that say about her? That she was a jinx.

The first had been her high school sweetheart, Billy Mays, who'd died in a head-on collision with a drunk man. The second had been when her husband, Jack, who'd died in a freak parasailing accident on their honeymoon in the US Virgin Islands. The third had been Patrick Jones, a man she'd only dated a few times. He'd died when he'd fallen off the big combine he'd been driving, and had been chopped into a hundred pieces before anyone could stop the combine.

Since then, she'd steered clear of relationships, hoping to spare any more deaths in the male population of Grizzly Pass, Wyoming. Which meant staying away from any entanglements with Caveman, the handsome Delta Force soldier who was only there on a temporary duty assignment. When he'd completed his assignment, he'd head back to his unit.

Wherever that was. Even if she wasn't cursed, a connection with Caveman wasn't possible.

This meant she had no right to be jealous of Melissa's flirting with Caveman. The waitress was welcome to him.

Yeah, maybe not. The woman could have the decency to wait until Grace wasn't around.

In the meantime, Grace would have his full attention. She might as well find out more about the man, to better understand the person who would be providing her personal protection until a murderer was caught and incarcerated.

She hoped that was sooner rather than later. It was hard to take a seat across the table from the soldier who made her pulse thunder. It reminded her of everything she'd been missing since she'd given up on men.

Chapter Six

Caveman leaned across the table and captured Grace's hand in his. He'd been watching her glancing right and left as if searching for an escape route from the booth. "Hey. I really don't bite."

She gave him a poor attempt at a smile. "Sorry. I guess I've been alone so much lately that being in a crowded room makes me antsy."

"Concentrate on the menu." He picked up one and opened it. "What are you going to have?"

"A bacon cheeseburger," she said without even looking. "They make the best."

"Sounds good." He closed the menu without having looked. "I'll have the same."

A harried waitress arrived and plunked two

cups of ice water on the table. "What can I get you to drink?"

"A draft beer for me."

"Me, too," Grace said. "And we're ready to order."

The waitress took their order and left, returning a few minutes later with two mugs filled with beer.

Caveman lifted his. "To finding a killer."

"Hear, hear." Grace touched her mug to his and drank a long swallow.

"I don't know too many women who like beer," Caveman said.

"And you say you're from Montana?" Grace snorted. "Lots of women drink beer around here."

He nodded. "It has been a while since I've been back in this area of the country. Hell, the world."

Grace set her mug on the table, leaned back and stared around the tavern. "Is it hard coming back?"

He nodded. "I feel like I have so much more to accomplish before I retire from the military."

"More battles to be fought and won?" Grace asked.

"Something like that." More like retribution for his brothers who'd lost their lives. He wanted to take out the enemy who'd lured them into an ambush and then slaughtered his teammates. Caveman shook his head and focused on Grace. "What about you? Are you from this area?"

She nodded. "Born and raised."

"Why don't you go live with your folks while the police search for the murderer?"

She laughed. "My work is here. My parents left Wyoming behind when my father retired from ranching. They live in a retirement community in Florida. They're even taking lessons on golfing."

"Are you an only child?"

A shadow crossed her face. "I am now."

"Sorry. I didn't mean to bring up bad memories."

"That's okay. It's been a long time. My little brother died of cancer when he was three. Leukemia."

"I'm so sorry."

"We all were. William was a ray of sunshine up to the very end. I believe he was stronger than all of us."

The waitress reappeared carrying two heaping plates. She set them on the table in front of them, along with a caddy of condiments. "If you need a refill, just wave me down. Enjoy."

She was off again, leaving Caveman and Grace to their meals.

Caveman gave himself over to the enjoyment of the best burger he'd ever tasted. "You weren't kidding," he said as he polished off the last bite. "I've never had a burger taste that good. What's their secret?"

"They grill them out back on a real charcoal grill. Even in the dead of winter, they have the grill going." Grace finished her burger and wiped the mustard off her fingers.

Caveman waved for the waitress and ordered two more draft beers and sat back to digest. "Do you mind my asking what happened to your husband?"

A shadow crossed her face and she pushed her fries around on her plate. "I told you, he died in a parasailing accident."

"You couldn't have been barely out of college six years ago."

"That's where we met. We were both studying biology. He went to work with Game and Fish, I landed a job with Yellowstone National Park. A match made in heaven," she whispered, her gaze going to the far corner of the room.

"That must have been hard. Was it on a lake around here?"

Her lips stretched in a sad kind of smile. "No, it was on our honeymoon in the Virgin Islands," she said, her voice matter-of-fact and emotionless.

Her words hit him square in the gut. "Wow. What a horrible ending to a new beginning." He covered her hand with his. "I'm sorry for your loss."

She stared at the top of his hand. "Like I said. It was a long time ago."

"You never remarried?"

She shook her head. "No."

"Didn't you say life goes on?"

"Yes, but that doesn't mean I had to go out and find another man to share my life. I'm content being alone."

Caveman wasn't dense. He could hear the finality of her statement. She wasn't looking for love from him or any other man. Which was a shame. She was beautiful in a natural, girl-next-door way. Not only was she pretty, she was intelligent and passionate about her work. A woman who was passionate about what she did had to be passionate in bed. At least that was Caveman's theory.

He found himself wondering just how passionate she could be beneath the sheets. His groin tightened and his pulse leaped at the thought. "You sound pretty adamant about staying alone. Don't you want to fall in love again?"

"No." She said that one word with emphasis. "Could we talk about something else?"

"Sure." He lifted his mug. "How about a toast to the next few days of togetherness."

"Okay. Let me." She raised her mug and tapped it against his, her gaze meeting his in an intense stare. "To keeping our relationship professional."

Caveman frowned. He didn't share her toast and didn't drink after she'd said the words. Though he knew he'd only be there until he got orders to return to his unit, he didn't discount the possibility of getting to know Grace better. And the more he was with her, the more he focused on the lushness of her lips and the gentle swell of her hips. This was a woman he could see himself in bed with, bringing out the same intensity of passion she displayed for her wolves.

Hell, he could see her as a challenge, one he'd meet head-on. Maybe she only *thought* she liked being alone. After a week with him, she might change her mind.

The thought of staying with her for the night evoked a myriad of images, none of which were professional or platonic. He had to remind himself that he was there to work, not to get too close to the woman he was tasked with protecting. She obviously had loved her husband. Six years after the man's death, she had yet to get over him.

He could swear he'd felt something when he touched her. An electric surge charging his blood, sending it pulsing through his body on a path south to pool low in his belly. Riding behind her on the ATV, his arms wrapped around her slim waist, he'd leaned in to sniff the fresh scent of her hair, the mountain-clean aroma reminding him of his home in Montana.

He'd take her to her house, make sure she got inside all right and then he'd sleep on the porch or on the couch. The woman was hands-off. He didn't need the complication a woman could become. Especially one with sandy-blond hair and eyes the gray of a stormy Montana sky.

They didn't talk much through the remainder of their dinner. Before long, they were on their way to her house, silence stretching between them. The thought of being with this desirable woman had Caveman tied in knots.

His fingers wrapped tightly around the steering wheel all the way to her house. When he pulled up in her drive, he wondered if he should just drop her off and leave. She had temptation written all over her, and he was a man who'd gone a long time without a woman. Grace was not the woman with whom to break that dry spell.

Chapter Seven

Caveman pulled up the driveway in front of Grace's house, shoved the gear into Park and climbed down from the truck.

Grace pushed her door open and was half-way out when he made it around the front of the truck to help her down. With his hand on her arm, he eased her to the ground. "How are you feeling?"

The color was high in her cheeks, but she answered, "Fine. Really. No dizziness or nausea. I don't see any reason for you to stay the night here. I'll lock the doors and sleep with my gun under my pillow."

He shook his head, the decision already made. "No use shooting your ear off. I'm staying."

She frowned, pulled the keys from her pocket and opened the door. "I can take—"

"I know. I know. You can take care of your-self." Hell, she'd given him the out he needed. Why was he arguing?

She unlocked the door and entered.

Caveman stopped her before she got too far ahead of him. "Do you mind if I have a look around before you get comfortable?" he asked.

"Are you going to do this every time we enter my house?" she asked.

He nodded. "Until the killer is caught."

"Be my guest." She stepped into the hallway and made room for him to pass.

He slipped by, pulled his gun from beneath his jacket and made a sweep of the house, checking all the rooms. By the time he'd re-turned from the back bedrooms, Grace had left the front hallway.

He followed sounds of cabinet doors open-ing and closing in the kitchen where he found Grace, nuking a couple of mugs in the micro-wave.

"I hope you like instant coffee or hot tea."

"Coffee. Instant is fine."

The microwave beeped and she pulled the mugs out, set them on the counter and plunked a tea bag in one of them. "I'd drink coffee, but

I don't want to be up all night. How do you do it?"

"Do what?"

"Sleep after drinking coffee?" she asked.

"You learn to sleep through almost anything when you're tired enough. Including a shot of caffeine."

She scooped a couple of spoonfuls of instant coffee into the hot water, dropped the spoon into the mug and set it on the kitchen table. Then she fished in the cupboard pulling out a bag of store-bought cookies. Carrying the cookies and her tea, she took the seat across from Caveman.

"So what's your story?" Grace dropped a teabag into her mug of hot water and dipped it several times.

The aroma of coffee and Earl Grey tea filled Caveman's nostrils and it calmed him without him actually having taken a sip. He inhaled deeply, took that sip and thought about her question.

Sitting in the comfort of her kitchen, the warm glow of the overhead light made the setting intimate somehow. Her gray-eyed gaze was soft and inviting, making him want to tell her everything there was to know about

Max Decker. But he wouldn't be around long enough to make it worth the effort. She was part of the job. He was going back to his unit soon. No use wasting time getting to know each other. "I don't have a story."

"We've already established that you're from Montana." She raised her tea to her lips and blew a stream of air at the liquid's surface.

The motion drew his attention to the sexiest part of her face—her lips. Or was it her eyes?

"It's not a secret." He lifted his mug and sipped on the scalding hot coffee, more for something to do. He really hadn't wanted the drink.

She tipped her head to the side. "What did you do before the military?"

Grace wasn't going to let him get away with short answers. He might as well get the interview over with. "Worked odd jobs after high school. But I left for the military as soon as I graduated college."

Her gaze dropped to the tea in her cup. "Married?"

Cavemen felt his lips tug upward at the corners. "No."

"Ever?" Grace met his gaze.

"Never."

"Never have?" Her eyes narrowed. "Or never will?"

"Both."

Grace lifted her mug to her lips and took a tentative sip of the piping hot liquid and winced. "How long have you been away from your unit?" she continued with the inquisition.

Caveman sighed. "Fourteen weeks, five days and thirteen hours."

"But who's counting?" Grace smiled, the gesture lighting her eyes and her face.

Wow. He hadn't realized just how pretty she was until that moment. Her understated beauty was that of an outdoorsy woman with confidence and intelligence.

"Some say you either love the military or hate it? Which side of the fence are you on?" she asked.

His chest swelled. "Yeah, there have been some really bad times, but being a part of the military has been like being a part of a really big family. It's a part of me."

"I'll take that as a 'Love it.'"

Turnabout was fair play. She didn't have the corner on the questions market. Caveman told himself, he wanted to learn more about her because the information might help him keep her safe. But that wouldn't be totally true. He really was interested in her answers. He leaned back in his seat. "What about you?"

GRACE STIFFENED. "NOPE. This interrogation is all about you. If I'm to trust you, I need to know more about you."

Caveman's lips quirked upward on the corners. "That's an unfair advantage."

"I never said I was fair. I am, however, nosy." She grinned and eased her mug onto the table to let the tea cool a little before she attempted another sip. "How are you with horses?"

He frowned. "Why?"

She pushed to her feet. "I need to feed and water my gelding. He's probably a little skittish after being shot at today." Grace started for the back door.

Caveman reached it before her. "You know, you put yourself in danger every time you step out into the open."

"I know, but I put my livestock in danger by not feeding or watering them. I'm going out to take care of my horse. You can come or finish your coffee. Your choice."

"Coming." He opened the door and stepped out on the porch. After a cursory glance in both directions, he waved her out onto the porch and slipped his arm around her. "Just stay close to me. Don't give a shooter an easy target."

As much as she hated to admit it, she liked the feel of Caveman's arm around her. Though she knew a shooter could kill them both, if he really wanted to, she felt safer with the man's body next to hers.

Inside the barn, Bear whinnied and pawed the stall door.

"I'm coming," Grace said. She scooped a bucket of grain from the feed bin, opened the stall door and stepped inside.

Caveman grabbed a brush and entered with her.

Bear's nostrils flared. He pawed the ground and tossed his head, as if telling Grace he wasn't pleased with the other human entering his domain.

"Bear doesn't like strangers."

Caveman didn't get the hint. Instead he stood in the stall with the brush in his hand, not moving or getting any closer to the horse.

Grace opened her mouth to ask Caveman to leave, but he started speaking soft, nonsensical words in a deep, calming tone.

Bear tossed his head several times, not easily won over, but he didn't paw the ground or snort his dissent. Soon the animal lowered his head and let Caveman reach out to scratch behind his ears.

"I'll be damned," Grace whispered.

Caveman covered Bear's ears. "Shh. Don't let that foulmouthed biologist scare you," he whispered.

The horse nuzzled the man's chest and leaned into the hand scratching his ear.

"So, not only are you a Delta Force soldier, you're a horse whisperer?" Grace snorted.

"I told you. I'm from Montana."

"And one of those odd jobs just happened to be on a ranch?"

He grinned. "Yes and no. I grew up on a ranch. I worked there during the summers for spending money."

"A cowboy. My mother warned me about getting involved with a cowboy."

"From what you said, your father was one."

"Exactly why she warned me." Though her mother was still crazy in love with her father, even after over thirty years of marriage.

"Why cowboys?" Caveman asked.

She met his gaze head-on. "They tend to like their horses better than their wives."

"Horses don't talk back as much, or make you fold laundry."

Grace chuckled. "I've had my share of sassy horses."

"Okay, so they don't make you clean the house."

"And I've cleaned my share of stalls." She crossed her arms over her chest and raised her eyebrows. "Care to try again?"

"I can sell a horse that's giving me a hard time, thus getting money for my trouble. Getting rid of a woman costs a heck of a lot more than ditching a horse."

"Okay, you got me on that one," Grace said. "But a horse won't be warming your bed and giving you children."

"Most of my married friends don't have sex more now that they're married. In fact, the kids suck the life out of their wives' sex drive."

"But your buddies have someone to come home to. People who care about them."

"Sometimes. Then there are the Dear John letters they get when in a hellhole fighting the enemy with their hands tied behind their backs by politicians. Meanwhile the wife back home has been having an affair with the banker next door."

Grace's brows rose. "Cynical much?"

Caveman shrugged. "I've seen some of the toughest soldiers commit suicide because they can't go home to salvage the relationship."

Caveman had worked himself up a rung on Grace's perception ladder with his horse trick. But she wasn't ready to fall for the big guy, yet. And despite her mother's warning not to fall for a cowboy, she had a soft spot in her heart for them, since her father had been one.

Hell, a man who had a way with animals, who'd been raised a cowboy, was a war hero and looked as good as Caveman could easily find his way beneath her defenses. If she wasn't careful, he might be the next victim of her curse.

Grace held out her hand. "I can take care of Bear."

He handed her the brush. "I'll haul the water."

"Not necessary. As soon as he's done eating, I'll let him out in the pasture. There's a trough in the paddock." She rounded the horse to the other side and went to work brushing his coat.

Caveman's presence raised the temperature of every blood cell in Grace's body. Fully aware of his every move, she knew when he left the stall. She let out a sigh and relaxed a little as she worked her way toward the horse's hindquarters.

The stall door squealed softly, announcing Caveman's return. He'd retrieved a currycomb and went to work on Bear's tangled mane and tail. Soon the horse was fully groomed, full of grain and ready to be turned loose in the pasture.

Yeah, the soldier had gone up another rung. Not every man would take the time to groom a horse. Not every man knew how to do it right.

She'd have to talk to Caveman's boss and ask him to send someone else. How would she approach the request? *Please send someone who isn't quite as drool-worthy. Maybe someone who is happily married, has a beer belly, belches in public and is not at all interesting.*

Grace hooked Bear's halter and led him through the barn and out to the gate.

Caveman moved ahead of her and had the gate open before she got there.

She let go of Bear's halter and the horse ran into the pasture, straight for the water trough.

Grace backed up, trying to get out of the

way of the gate. Her foot caught on the uneven ground and she tipped backward.

Caveman caught her in his arms and hauled her up against his chest. "Are you all right?"

No, she wasn't. Cinched tightly to the man's chest, she could barely breathe, much less think. She tried to tell herself that the malfunctioning of her involuntary reflexes had nothing to do with how close Caveman was to her. Neither were his arms, which were hooked beneath her breasts, causing all kinds of problems with her pulse and blood pressure. "I'm fine. Seriously, you can let go of me."

For a long moment, he stared down at her, his arms unmoving. "Anyone ever tell you that your eyes sparkle in the moonlight?"

And there went any measure of resistance. "No." Whether her one-word answer was in response to his question or in response to her rising desire, she refused to pick it apart.

"They do," he said. "And your lips clearly were made to be kissed."

Her heart hammering against her ribs, Grace watched as Caveman lowered his head, his mouth coming so close to hers she could feel the warmth of his breath on her skin. She tipped her head upward, her eyelids, sweeping low, her pulse racing. Dear Lord, he was going to kiss her. And she was going to let him!

A BREATH AWAY from touching his mouth to hers, Caveman came to his senses. What was he thinking? This woman had nearly died that day. He was responsible for her safety, not for making a pass at her. As much as he wanted to kiss her, he shouldn't. It would compromise his ability to remain objective. Then why had he mentioned how her eyes sparkled and how her lips were meant to be kissed?

Because, man! He wanted to kiss her. With a deep sigh, he untangled his arms from around her.

Grace opened her eyes and blinked. Even in the moonlight, Caveman could see the color rise in her cheeks. She stepped out of his reach, careful not to trip again, straightened her blouse and nodded. "Thanks for catching me. In the future, I'll do my best not to fall."

As she headed back to the house, he followed closely behind her, using his body as a shield. Should the shooter decide to follow her to her home, he wouldn't have a clear target. He'd have to go through Caveman first.

Once inside the house, Grace gathered a

blanket and pillow, handed them to him and pointed to the couch. "You can stay on the couch."

The couch beat his truck and the front porch, but it might still be too close.

Grace disappeared into the only bathroom in the house.

Caveman could hear the sound of the shower and his imagination went wild, picturing the beautiful biologist stripping out of her clothes, stepping into the shower and water running in rivulets down her naked body.

He left the blanket on the couch and slipped out onto the front porch. Yeah, sleeping on the hard, wood planks with a solid wood door locked between them would be the right thing to do. Knowing she'd be in the bed down the hall made his groin tight and guaranteed he wouldn't sleep any better than the night before when he'd caught a few hours cramped in the front seat of his truck.

Tomorrow, he'd speak with Kevin about assigning another one of the team members to watch over Grace. Apparently, he'd been too long without a woman. What else would make him so attracted to Grace when he'd only known her a few hours?

The door behind him opened and Grace stuck her head through the screen door. "The shower's all yours."

She wore a baggy T-shirt that hung halfway down her thighs. If she had on shorts, the shirt covered them. And when she turned to the side, her shirt stretched over her chest.

Caveman sucked in a breath and his jeans got even tighter.

She wasn't wearing a bra beneath the shirt. The beaded tips of her nipples made tiny tents against the fabric.

What had she said? Oh, yes. The shower was all his. He really should have told her he didn't need one and that he would sleep outside. But no, that might require more explanation than he was prepared to give. And it might scare her to think the man who was supposed to protect her wanted to jump her bones. "I'll be there in a minute."

"Okay." She started to turn, paused and then faced him. "Thank you for rescuing me today."

"You're welcome." *Now, go straight to your bedroom and lock your door.* Caveman clenched his fists to keep from reaching out and dragging her into his arms. "Have a good night," he said, his voice huskier than usual.

Again, she started to turn, changed her mind
and stepped through the door, closed the distance between them. When she stood in front
of him, she raised up on her toes and brushed
her lips across his cheek. Before Caveman
could react, Grace turned and ran back into
the house.

He groaned and adjusted the tightness of his
jeans. Yeah, he wouldn't get much sleep. When
he could move comfortably again, he walked
out to his truck, grabbed his duffel bag from
the backseat and returned to the house, locking the front door behind him. He made another pass through the house, checking all of
the doors and windows with the exception of
Grace's bedroom.

When he was certain the house was locked
down, he entered the bathroom, shucked his
clothes and turned on the cold water. After
several minutes beneath the icy spray, he was
back in control, his head on straight and his
resolve strengthened.

Grace Saunders was off-limits. Period. End
of subject.

He lay on the couch, his gun close by, and
stared at the ceiling for the next few hours. Finally, in the wee hours of the morning he fell

asleep and dreamed of making love to a beautiful, sandy-blond-haired biologist who loved wolves. Even in his dream, he knew he was treading the fine line of professionalism, but he couldn't resist. The crow of a rooster jolted him away as the gray light of predawn edged through the window.

He had breakfast on the table by the time Grace emerged from her bedroom.

"You're kind of handy to have around." She yawned and stretched. "Not only do you rescue damsels in distress, you can scramble eggs? You'll make someone a great wife."

"Don't get used to it. I cooked out of self-defense." He handed her one of the two places of fluffy yellow eggs. "I was starving."

She smiled and padded barefoot to the table. "What's the plan for today?"

"I thought we'd stop by the tavern and see if Kevin and his computer guy have come up with any potential murder suspects."

"You think they might have more than the sheriff and his deputies have come up with?"

"Hack, Kevin's computer guy, is a pretty talented techie. He's been following up on the Vanders family and their connections in the community. He might have found someone who was as trigger-happy as the Vanders."

Grace chewed on a bite of toast and swallowed. "What's wrong with people? In the past, all we had to complain about was the weather and taxes. Now people are shooting at each other. Last night all I could think about was Mr. Khalig's family. Did he leave a wife and children behind? People who loved him and looked forward to his return?"

Her face was sad, making Caveman want to wrap his arms around her and make everything okay. But he couldn't. No amount of hugging would bring back a dead man. Hugging was a bad idea, anyway. He'd promised himself that he'd steer clear of temptation.

Caveman looked down to keep from staring at Grace's sad eyes. He poked his fork at his eggs. "Not everyone is bad or crazy."

"You're right." She chuckled. "I was lucky enough one of the good guys was there when I needed someone." She ate the rest of her eggs and toast with a gusto most women didn't demonstrate.

Caveman finished his breakfast, as well. When he reached for her plate, she held up her hand. "I'll take care of the dishes since you cooked." She took his plate to the sink, and filled it with water and soapsuds.

Having grown up on a ranch where his mother worked outside as much as his father did, Caveman couldn't stand by and not help. He grabbed a dry dish towel and stepped up beside Grace. "You wash, I'll dry. We'll get it done in no time."

She smiled, and it seemed like the sun chose that moment to shine through the window.

Caveman forced himself to focus on the dish in his hand, not the sun in Grace's hair.

When they were done, and the dishes were stacked neatly in the cabinet, Grace disappeared into her bedroom and came out wearing boots and a jacket, her hair brushed neatly and pulled back into a ponytail.

Caveman liked her hair hanging down around her shoulders, the long straight strands like silver-gold silk swaying back and forth with each step. Lord help him, he was waxing poetic in his head. His buddies back in his unit would have a field day if they knew. "Come on. We need to stop by the sheriff's office and give him your official statement and see what else they can tell us about the shootings."

"I hope they were able to retrieve Mr. Khalig's body."

Caveman stepped out on the porch and searched the tree line and shadows for movement before he allowed Grace out of the house. "I spoke briefly with Kevin on the phone. They did. He's with the coroner in Jackson. They'll provide a report as soon as they can."

Grace locked the front door and followed Caveman to the truck.

Within ten minutes, they were inside the sheriff's office.

Grace gave her statement. The sheriff recorded the session and made notes. When she was done, he stared across the table at her. "I'd like to think you'll be okay. Since you didn't see who it was, you can't identify the shooter. For your sake, I hope he lays low and leaves you alone."

"I wish I *had* seen him. I'd rather know and be hunted than not know. As it is, it could have been anyone." She pushed to her feet.

The sheriff did too and held out his hand.

She ignored the hand and hugged the older man. "Thank you, for all you do. Give your wife my love."

Caveman felt a stab of envy for the hug the sheriff was getting from the pretty biologist.

Sheriff Scott hugged her back and patted her back. "You be careful out there. Can't have our favorite wolf lady getting hurt."

Caveman gave his brief statement of how he'd found Grace and thanked the sheriff.

"Where to?"

"Operations Center," Caveman said, a little more brusquely than he intended. That jolt of envy for a friendly hug Grace had given the sheriff had set Caveman off balance. He barely knew Grace. Perhaps the hit he'd taken to his leg and all the morphine he'd had during the operation and recovery had scrambled his wits. He needed to get his head on straight. Soon. He wasn't going to be around long enough to get to know the woman, nor was he in the market for a long-term relationship. He had a unit to get back to.

But the sway of Grace's hips, and the way she smiled with her lips and her eyes, seemed to replay in his head like a movie track stuck in replay mode.

By the time they had debriefed Kevin and Hack, the computer guru, they'd missed lunch and the evening crowd had begun to gather at the tavern below.

"Want to grab something to eat before we head back to my house?" Grace's lips twisted into a wry grin. "I don't cook often, and I'm certain it was a fluke you actually found something in the refrigerator for breakfast."

"Sure," Caveman said. "Then we can stop at the store for some groceries, if it's still open when we're done."

"I'm game."

For the second time in the past two days, Caveman and Grace entered the tavern and asked for a seat in the dining area.

"If you ever want to find out what's going on, you need to people-watch in the tavern or go to the grocery store. Mrs. Penders knows all of the gossip."

"Then we're definitely going to the store next."

"Hi, Grace, good to see you again. Who's this?"

Grace smiled at a pretty, young waitress with bleach-blond hair. "Lisa Lambert, this is Max Decker. You can call him Caveman. He's a…friend of mine."

Lisa grinned. "Caveman? Is that a statement

on how you are with the ladies?" She winked. "Nice to meet you." She held out a hand.

Caveman shook it, and gave Lisa a smile. "Nice to meet you, Lisa."

"You know, if it's all the same to you," Grace said. "I'd like to get the food to go and eat it at home."

"We can do that," Lisa said. She took their order and hurried to the back. She returned a few minutes later with two glasses of water and a smile. "The cook said it will take him ten minutes."

"Great." After Lisa left, Caveman leaned toward Grace. "See anyone here that might be your killer?"

She glanced around the room. "I see a bunch of people I've known all my life. I find it hard to believe any of them could be a killer. I grew up with some of them, went to church on Sunday with others and say hello to others at community functions."

"Anyone who might have a beef with the pipeline inspector?"

Grace studied the people. "Some of the men worked on the pipeline. Maybe the ones who were laid off are angry because Mr. Khalig still had his job? I don't know. I work with wolves, not pipeline workers."

"What about the property owners the pipelines cross?" Caveman asked.

"Maybe. I'm not sure who they are, though. The pipelines cross the entire state. Mr. Khalig was on federal land when he was shot."

A few minutes later, Lisa returned with a bag filled with two covered plates.

Handing her several bills, Caveman told her to keep the tip. He had turned to leave when he heard a commotion behind him.

"I don't care what you say!" a slurred male voice yelled over the sound of other patrons talking.

Caveman spun toward the bar to see a man leaning with his back to the bar. "The BLM isn't a law unto themselves. You have no right to confiscate a man's herd or have him arrested for trespassing on the land his cattle have grazed on since his great-great-grandfather settled this area."

"If the man doesn't pay the grazing fees for his animals, and he doesn't remove them from federal property, he forfeits them to the government," another man said, his voice lower. "It's in the contract he signed."

A pause in general conversation allowed Caveman to hear the man's quiet response. "Who are the two arguing?"

"The man at the bar is Ernie Martin," Grace said. "He poured all his money into raising Angora goats, counting on the subsidies the government gave ranchers for raising them. The subsidies were cut from the federal budget, and now he's facing bankruptcy."

"And the other guy?" Caveman prompted.

"Daryl Bradley. He's a local Bureau of Land Management representative. They sent him in to feed information to the agency on how it's going out here. They had a man who wouldn't pay his grazing fees try to shoot the sheriff. It's been pretty volatile out here. *You* should know. I heard you had a hand in rescuing the school bus full of kids just the other day."

He nodded. "Vanders was the man who tried to shoot the sheriff. And it was his sons who kidnapped the kids. That could have turned out a whole lot worse than it did."

Grace nodded. "It was bad enough old Mr. Green died. He was a good man."

Caveman nodded. "Thankfully, all of the kids survived."

Grace shook her head. "I never would have

thought members of our little community could be that desperate they could kill a kind old man and kidnap a bunch of innocent kids."

"It ain't right," Ernie shouted. "How's a man supposed to make a living when the government is out to squeeze every ounce of blood from his livelihood? The land doesn't cost the government anything to maintain. *We* fix the fences. *We* provide the water and feed for the cattle. And the BLM collects the money. For what? To fund some pork belly program nobody wants or needs."

"The BLM hasn't raised the fees in years," Daryl said. "We haven't even kept up with inflation. It was time."

"That's taxation without representation. Our forefathers dumped tea in a harbor to protest the government raising taxes without them having a say in it." Ernie slammed his mug on the bar, sloshing beer over the top. "It's time we take back our country, the land our grandfathers fought to protect, and boot the likes of you out."

Daryl stood, pushing back his chair so hard it tipped over and crashed to the floor. "Is that a threat?"

"Call it whatever you want," Ernie shouted.

"It's time we took matters into our own hands and set things straight in the US."

A tall, slender man rose from his chair and ambled over to the fray. "Oh, pipe down, Ernie. You're just mad because they cut the government subsidies for Angora goats."

Grace leaned close to Caveman. "That's Ryan Parker. Owns the Circle C Ranch."

"Yeah, you're right, I'm mad." Ernie poked a finger toward Ryan. "I sold my cattle to invest in those damned goats. It's like they timed it perfectly to close me down. I've already had to sell half of my land. It won't be long before I sell the other half, just to pay my mortgage and taxes." He puffed out his chest. "The government has to understand the decisions they make affect real people."

"That's why we go to the voting booths and elect the representatives who will take our message to Washington." Ryan waved toward the door. "Go home, Ernie."

"And what good will voting do?" Ernie shouted. "You're not in much better shape. What has our government done for you? You had to sell most of your breeding stock to make ends meet. How are you going to recover from that? Not only that, you didn't have a choice on that pipeline cutting through your property. What if it breaks? What if it leaks? Your remaining livestock could be poisoned, the land ruined for grazing."

"Or we could all die in the next volcanic eruption. We can't predict the future." Ryan crossed his arms over his chest. "No one made you sell all of your livestock to invest the money in goats. Any ranch owner worth his salt knows not to put all his eggs in one basket."

"So now you're saying I'm not worth my salt?" Ernie marched across the floor and stood toe-to-toe with Ryan.

Caveman tensed and extended a hand to Grace. "Might be getting bad in here. Are you ready to go?"

Her gaze was riveted on the two men shouting at each other. "Think we should do anything to stop them?"

"My job is to protect *you*, not break up a barroom fight."

"I didn't go to war to fight for your right to collect subsidies from our government." Ryan glared down at Ernie. "You made a bad financial decision. Live with it."

"Why, you—" Ernie swung his fist.

Ryan Parker caught it in his palm and shoved it back at him. "Don't ever take a swing at me again. I won't let it go next time."

Ernie spat on Ryan's cowboy boots. "You're one of them."

"And if you mean I'm a patriot who loves my country and fought to keep it free for dumbasses like you, then yes. I'm one of them. What have you done for your country lately, Ernie?"

Ernie rubbed his fist. If his glare was a knife it would have skewered Ryan through the heart. "I might not have joined the military, but I'm willing to fight for my rights."

"And what rights are those? The right to raise goats at the taxpayer's expense?" Ryan shook his head. "Get a real life, Ernie. One that you've earned, not one that you've gambled on and lost."

Ernie's face turned a mottled shade of red. He reached into his pocket, his eyes narrowing into slits.

Grace started toward the man before Caveman realized what she was doing.

He leaped forward and grabbed her arm, pulling her back behind him.

"But Ernie's going to do something stupid," Grace said. "Ryan's one of the good guys."

"I'll handle it," Caveman said between clenched teeth. "Stay out of it," he ordered and strode toward the angry man.

"You'll see." Ernie eased his hand out of his pocket, something metal and shiny cupped in his palm. Based on the size and shape, it had to be a knife. "You and every other governmental tyrant will see. Just you wait, Parker." Ernie's brows drew together and he took a step toward Ryan. "You'll see. We'll have a free America again. And it won't be because you went to fight in a foreign country. We'll bring the fight back home where it belongs."

"What do you mean?" Ryan stood his ground.

Caveman also wanted to know what the belligerent Ernie meant by bringing the fight home, but he wasn't willing to wait for the angry drunk to explain.

Ernie started forward, cocked his arm, preparing to thrust his hand at Ryan.

Caveman popped Ernie's wrist with his fist in a short, fast impact that caused the man to drop the knife. "Sorry. Didn't mean to bump into you," he said and kicked the knife beneath a table, out of Ernie's reach.

Clenching his empty hand into a fist, Ernie glared at Caveman and then turned his attention back to Ryan. "It won't be long. And you'll see."

Two other men stepped between Ernie and Ryan. "You've said enough," one of the men muttered.

"That's fine." Ernie snorted. "I'm done here." He turned toward the door and pushed his way through the crowd that had gathered around him and Ryan. "Move. Get out of my way."

As the tavern returned to its normal dull roar of voices, Caveman made his way back to where he'd left Grace. "What was Ernie talking about, *bringing the fight back home?*"

Grace's brow formed a V over her nose. "I'm not sure. We've heard rumblings about a militia group forming in the area. But that's the first I've heard anyone actually talk about bringing the fight here." She glanced around as if looking at the crowd with fresh eyes.

"Who were the guys who stopped Ernie?" Caveman looked for the men, but didn't see them. They'd disappeared into the crowd and Ryan had stepped up to the bar to pay his bill.

"That was Quincy Kemp and Wayne Batson. Quincy was the one who spoke to Ernie. He's not the nicest or most reputable individual in Grizzly Pass. But he does make good sausage. All of the hunters go to him to have their antlers mounted and the meat turned into steaks, sausage or jerky."

"He's a butcher *and* a taxidermist?" Caveman asked.

"Yes. He has a shop in town, but he lives off the grid. His home is up in the hills. He uses wind and solar power and hunts for his food."

"Pretty good shot?"

"I'd say he'd have to be to feed himself and his family." Her lips pulled up on the corner. "As for Wayne Batson, he nearly went bankrupt when ranching got too expensive. He sank a lot of money into making his place a sportsman's paradise, building high fences around his ten-thousand-acre ranch and stocking it with exotic deer, elk, wolves and wildcats. He also has one of the most sophisticated outdoor rifle ranges in the state. Men come to train on his range and hunt on his land."

"Maybe we should ask the sheriff to check their alibis."

"Wayne and Quincy are highly skilled hunters." Grace smiled. "But, if we were looking for the best hunters in the area as our potential shooter, you'd have to question half the people in this county alone. You know how it is. Most men in these parts grew up with a guns in their hands. They're all avid hunters and are good with a rifle and scope. We even have a man from here who became the state champion rifle marksman."

"You're right. It was the same in Montana. I guess I've been in other parts of this country too long, where most people wouldn't know how to load a gun, much less shoot one."

"Most of them don't need one to survive." She gathered her purse. "We should go. I need to log my notes into the project database and notify my boss of the loss of Loki."

Normally, Caveman would have held the door for Grace, but he wanted to go out first and scan the parking lot for danger before he allowed her to leave the relative security of the tavern.

He stopped in the doorway and looked around.

Three men stood near a truck talking in hushed voices, their faces intense. One of them was Ernie Martin. The other men had their backs to Caveman, but based on the one's greasy brown hair and slouchy blue jeans, he appeared to be Quincy Kemp, the local meat processor and taxidermist. The other had the swaggering stance of the man Grace had called Wayne Batson.

"What's going on," Grace asked, her breath warming Caveman's shoulder, sending a thrill of awareness through him.

"Ernie, Wayne and Quincy are having a conversation."

"I'm not afraid of them," she said.

He looked around for any other threats. The sun had set and the gray of dusk provided enough light to make their way to their truck, but not enough to see into the shadows. "Stay close to me. When we get to the truck, get in and stay down. Don't provide any kind of silhouette."

"I'm still not quite convinced the shooter is actually after me anymore. He has to know by now that I couldn't identify him. Otherwise someone would have been knocking at his door."

"That doesn't mean he won't take pleasure in keeping you guessing. A man who'd hang a dead wolf's collar on your door might go to the trouble of continuing to scare you." Caveman handed her up into the passenger seat. "Even if you're not scared of him, I might be. For you, of course." He winked, his hand on the door. "Again, stay down until we're back at your house."

She rolled her eyes, but complied, doubling over in her seat, bringing her head below the dash, out of sight of any passerby, or shooter aiming at the truck.

Caveman climbed into the truck, started the engine and pulled out of the Blue Moose parking lot onto the road headed toward Grace's house.

Chapter Eight

"I feel silly bending over this long." Grace lay over, her face near the sack of food, the smells making her mouth water. "Are we there yet? My stomach is rumbling."

"Rather silly than sorry," he said.

"Easy for you to say. You're not the one scrunched over your seat." She straightened for a moment and worked the kink out of her neck. "Seriously, this is nuts. I went all day without anyone making a move. Nobody is going to shoot at me at night."

A sharp tink sounded and a hole appeared in the passenger seat window a few inches away from Grace's head. "What the hell?" She reached out her hand to touch the round hole. Splinters of glass flaked off at her touch.

"Get down!" Caveman yelled and swerved into the middle of the road.

Someone was shooting at them! Caveman jerked, his hand, twisting the steering wheel to the right. He cursed and held on, straightening the truck before he plowed into a ditch and flipped the vehicle.

Caveman steadied the vehicle, slammed his foot on the accelerator and sped forward. When he glanced at the matching holes in the window, his heart stopped for a second. Those were bullet holes. Had Grace been leaning a few inches forward in her seat, those bullets would have hit her in the head.

His gut clenched.

Grace lay doubled over, her head between her knees to keep from being seen by the enemy. "Should we go straight to the sheriff's office?" she asked from her bent position.

"Probably, but I'm not sure what that will accomplish since the sheriff will have gone home by now," Caveman said.

"Should we go to my house? We could call the sheriff from there." The shooter already knew where she lived and had been there the day before.

"Is there anywhere else we could go?" Caveman asked.

Grace shook her head. "We could drive up to the park at Yellowstone and see if they can fit us into one of the cabins."

"And if they can't?" Caveman glanced across the console at her.

"We could drive on into Jackson Hole. There's bound to be a hotel there."

"That's a lot of driving late at night."

"Then we go to my place," she decided. "I don't like leaving my horse for too long, anyway. If this guy shoots wolves, he doesn't have a sense of compassion in dealing with animals. He could decide to hurt my horse."

"Almost there," Caveman pulled into her driveway and shone the headlights at her small cottage. Nothing seemed amiss. Then he drove around the side of the house and shone the headlights at the small barn. The lights reflected off the horse's eyes, but everything appeared normal.

He parked at the rear of the house.

"I know," Grace said. "I'm to stay put while you check it out." She sighed. "I'm sorry about your window."

"Don't worry about it. I'm glad you weren't

hit." He pushed open the door to his truck. The overhead light illuminated Grace's pale face and worried eyes.

He reached over and touched a hand to her cheek, wanting to take her into his arms, as if by doing so he could protect her from whoever was shooting at her. "If you had any doubts the shooter is after you, I hope you're convinced now."

"I am," she said, quietly. "Completely." She covered his hand with hers and leaned into his palm. "But why? I still don't have a clue who it is. It's not like I'm a threat to him."

"Doesn't matter at this point. What does matter is that we get you inside that house safely before the gunman has the chance to get here from his previous location."

"Caveman?"

"Yeah."

"Thanks for being here for me."

Caveman pressed his lips together. "Don't thank me until the gunman is caught." She was still in danger and he could be the best body-guard around, but a skilled sniper could take someone out from up to four hundred yards away.

He wasn't sure what they'd do next. He

didn't see any other option but to stay inside the house, avoid all the windows and pray whoever was shooting wouldn't get lucky and hit Grace. Though he'd only known her a very short time, he wouldn't want anything to happen to the dedicated biologist.

Chapter Nine

Grace felt strange running for the door of her house. This was Grizzly Pass, Wyoming, not some village in a war-torn nation. People didn't shoot at you for no reason.

Unless you witnessed a murder, and the killer was crazier than a rabid skunk, and fired on you when you were driving home from town.

Ducking low, Grace ran up the porch steps.

Caveman was right behind her, using his body as a shield to protect hers, again. Was he insane?

When her hand shook too much to insert the key in the lock, Caveman took the key from her and opened the door. With his palm on the small of her back, he hurried her through and closed the door behind them.

She rounded on him, realizing too late that she hadn't given him much room to get in the door and close it. She stood toe-to-toe with the man, feeling the heat radiating off his body. "Why do you keep doing that?"

He raised his hands to cup her elbows. "Doing what?"

"Using your body to shield mine? You don't have to take a bullet for me." She touched his arm. "You hardly know me."

He gave her a half smile. "Let's just say, what I know, I like and admire." His lips twitched and his eyes twinkled. "You're the first woman I've met who likes beer. What's not to love about you?"

Her heart warmed at his playful words. If she wasn't such a deadly jinx, she'd be tempted to flirt with the man. "Well, don't do it, again. I don't think I could live with myself if something happened to you because of me." She set her purse on the hall table and would have walked away, but Caveman took her hand and laced his fingers with hers.

"Sweetheart, I'm here to protect you. I'm not going to leave you exposed to a sniper's sights."

"I'm not your sweetheart, and you should

wear a bulletproof vest if you're going to be around me." She stared up into his eyes, her own stinging. Her chest ached with an overwhelming fear for his life. "I don't want to be the cause of another death."

"You have to stop beating yourself up." He raised her hand to his lips, pressed a kiss to her knuckles and sent sparks shooting through her veins. "Khalig didn't die because of you."

"I know." She stared at where his lips had been. She wished he would claim her mouth instead of wasting kisses on her fingers. But, no, that wouldn't work. Grace shook her head. "I can't do this to you."

"Do what?"

"Nothing." She pulled her hand free and turned away.

Caveman caught her arm and pulled her around to face him. "Do what to me?" He cupped her cheek in his palm. "Drive me crazy? Too late. For some reason, I'm insanely attracted to you. But every time I think I'm about to kiss you, you pull away, or my head gets screwed on straight. Well, I'm tired of doing the right thing. I swear your eyes are saying yes, but the next thing I know, you're running. Is it something I said? Is it my cologne? I'll change it."

Grace rested her hand on his chest as tears welled in her eyes. "Don't say nice things. Don't try to kiss me."

"Why not?" He brushed his thumb across her lips. "You're beautiful. And I might be reading too much into your body language, but I think you want to kiss me, too."

Yes, she did. But now, she couldn't. "I can't do this to you."

He stepped closer, bringing his body nearer to hers, the warmth crushing her ability to resist. "Can't do what to me? Talk to me, Grace. You're not making sense."

"I can't curse you."

He leaned his head back, his brows forming a V in the center of his forehead. "Curse me? I don't understand."

"I'm cursed. If you kiss me, I'll jinx you. I don't want something terrible to happen to you." She curled her fingers into his shirt, knowing she should push him away, but she couldn't. Now that they were so close, her brain stopped thinking and her body took over. She wanted, more than anything, for him to kiss her.

"Let me get this straight. You think that by kissing me, you'll jinx me?" He stared down at her for a long moment. Finally, he said, "What in the Sam-dog-hell are you talking about?"

Her brows lifted and her lips twitched. "Sam-dog-hell?" She gave a shaky laugh.

"Don't change the subject." He brushed his thumb across her lips again, his glance shifting to his thumb's path. "I was just about to kiss you."

"I didn't change the subject. And you can't kiss me." She was saying one thing while she allowed him to tip her chin up, her lips coming to within a breath of his. "Kissing me is a really bad idea," she whispered.

"Damn it, Grace, if kissing you is a bad idea, then color me bad. I have to do it." He bent to claim her lips. "Curses be damned," he muttered into her mouth, sliding his tongue between her teeth, claiming her tongue with a warm, wet caress that curled Grace's toes.

She pressed her body against his, longing to be closer, their clothes just one more barrier to overcome so that she could be skin-to-skin with this big soldier who'd take a bullet for a relative stranger. What had she done to deserve him?

Nothing. So how could she stand there kissing him, knowing it would put him in mortal danger? Grace pushed against his chest, though the effort was only halfhearted and less than convincing.

His arms tightened and then loosened. "If you really want me to let go, just say the word." He stared down into her eyes. "Otherwise, I'm going to continue kissing you."

She fell into his gaze, her heart hammering against her ribs. Slowly, her hands slid up his chest to lock behind his head, pulling him down for that promised kiss. "If you die, I'll never forgive myself."

He chuckled. "I'll take my chances." Then he kissed her until her insides tingled and she forgot the need to breathe. When he raised his head, she lowered her hands to the buttons on his shirt, working them loose as fast as her fingers could push them through the holes. Her goal was to get to the skin beneath, before her brain kicked in and reminded her why she shouldn't be kissing him and whatever else might come next.

As she reached for the rivet on his blue jeans, he captured her hands in his. "Are you sure about this? You know I want it, but I don't want you to do something you'll regret later."

She caught her lower lip between her teeth and stared down at the button on his jeans, wishing he hadn't stopped her, praying her brain wouldn't kick in. "You're a soldier, right?" she said.

"Yes. So?"

"You've lived through some pretty serious battles, I assume?"

"Again, yes."

"You can take care of yourself, right?"

"I can."

"Then kiss me and tell me you'll be all right."

"Grace, no one is guaranteed to live to old age." He threaded his hands through her hair. "We have to live every day like it could be our last."

"Yeah, but I don't want your life to be cut short because of me."

"Let *me* make that choice. The only decision you need to make is whether you want to make love here, against the wall or take it to the bedroom?"

Her pulse raced, and her breathing grew ragged. "Here. Now." She ripped open the button on his jeans and dragged the zipper down.

Caveman grabbed the hem of her shirt, pulled it up over her head and dropped it on the hall table. Then he bent to kiss her neck, just below her ear. He nibbled at her earlobe and trailed his lips down the length of her neck. Continuing lower, he tongued the swell of her right breast, while pushing the strap over her shoulder and down her arm.

Past anything resembling patience, Grace reached behind her and unclipped her bra. Her breasts freed, she shrugged out of the garment and it fell to the floor.

Caveman cupped both orbs in his hands and plumped them, thumbing the nipples until they hardened into tight little beads. He bent to take one into his mouth, sucking it deep, then flicking it with the tip of tongue.

Grace moaned and arched her back, wanting so much more. They still had too many clothes on. She shoved her hands into the back of his jeans, cupped his bottom and pulled him close. His shaft sprang free of his open fly and pushed into her belly.

"I want to feel your skin against mine," he said, his words warm on her wet breast.

"What's holding you back?" she managed to get out between ragged gasps.

"These." He flipped the button of her jeans through the hole and dragged the denim down her legs. Dropping to his haunches, he pulled off her cowboy boots and helped her step free. As he rose, he skimmed his knuckles along her inner thigh, all the way up to the triangle of silk covering her sex.

His gaze met hers as he hooked the elastic waistband of her panties and he dragged them over her hips and down her thighs.

Her body on fire, Grace couldn't take it anymore. She pushed his jeans down his legs and waited for him to toe off his boots, kicking them to the side. He shucked his pants, pulling his wallet from the back pocket before he slung them against the wall. Then they were both naked in the hallway of her home.

A cool waft of air almost brought her back to her senses.

Before it could, Caveman retrieved a condom from his wallet, tossed the wallet on the hallway table and handed her the packet. "We might need that."

"I'm glad *someone* is thinking," she said. She sure wasn't. Grace tore open the foil, rolled the condom over his engorged shaft all the way to the base. Sweet heaven, he was hard, long and so big, her breath caught and held.

Caveman tipped her chin and brushed a light kiss over her lips, then scooped her up by the backs of her thighs and wrapped her legs around his waist. Pinning her wrists to the wall above her head, he pressed his shaft to her damp entrance. "Slow and easy, or hard and fast?"

Her eyes widened. No man had ever asked her how she liked it. Not even her husband. She assumed it was up to the guy to establish the pace.

She only took a moment to decide. With her body on fire, her channel slick and ready, there was only one choice. "Hard and fast."

He eased into her, let her adjust to his thickness and then pulled out. Dropping his grip on her wrists, Caveman held her hips, his fingers digging into the flesh. Soon, he was pumping in and out of her, moving faster and faster, their movements making thumping sounds against the wall.

Grace held on to his shoulders, her head tipped back, her breath lodged in her chest as wave after wave of sensations ebbed through her, consuming her in a massive firestorm of desire. When she thought it couldn't get any better, he hit the sweet spot and sent her catapulting over the edge. She held on, riding him to the end.

One last thrust and he drove deep inside, pressing her firmly against the wall, his staff throbbing inside her. He leaned his forehead against hers, his breaths short and fast, like a marathon runner's.

A minute passed, and then two.

Grace didn't care, she teetered on the brink of a euphoric high. He could do it all again, and she'd be perfectly happy.

Caveman tightened his hold around her and carried her into the master bedroom, where he laid her on the bed. In the process, he lost their connection.

Grace ached inside, the emptiness leaving her cold. But not for long.

He slipped onto the mattress behind her and pulled her back to his front. His still-hard shaft nudged her between her legs and pressed against her entrance, sliding easily inside. Slipping his arms around her, he held her close, driving the chill from the air and her body.

She could be content to lie with him forever. After making love against the wall and being completely pleased, she could imagine how much more satisfying making love in the comfort of a bed might be.

If he stayed with her through the night, she vowed to find out before morning.

Pushing all the niggling thoughts of her curse to the back of her mind, she snuggled closer, giving him time to recuperate before she tested his ability to perform more than once in a night.

A CURSE. CAVEMAN had wanted to laugh off Grace's mention of it, but she'd been very adamant to the point she'd held him at arm's length. Until she couldn't fight the attraction another minute. He felt a twinge of guilt for teasing her into abandoning her cause and making love to him.

"So why is it you think I will be cursed?" he said, nuzzling the back of her ear.

She stiffened in his arms.

Caveman could have kicked himself for bringing it up after the most amazing sex he'd had in a very long time. "Never mind. I'm not very superstitious, anyway."

For a long time, she lay silent in his arms.

He began to think she'd gone to sleep.

"My high school sweetheart died in a head-on collision the night after I lost my virginity to him," she said. "He was eighteen."

Caveman kissed the curve of her shoulder. "Could have happened to anyone."

"That's what I thought." She inhaled deeply and let it out. "My husband died on our honeymoon. The day after we got there. We went parasailing. The cable holding his chute to the boat broke. He had no way to control the parachute. It slammed him into a cliff and he crashed to the rocks below. He was only twenty-four."

"Just because two of the guys you cared about died doesn't mean you are cursed."

She snorted softly. "A couple years ago, I decided to get back into the dating scene. I met a nice man. We dated three times. After our third date, I didn't hear from him for a few days. I called his cell phone number. A woman answered. I asked where he was. She broke down and cried, saying he'd died in a farming accident."

"Grace, you can't blame yourself for their deaths. Sometimes your number is just up. Those cases were all unrelated and coincidental."

"No, they were related. I cared about all

three of them. The common denominator was me." She eased away from him, turned and faced him, her head lying on the pillow, her hand falling to his chest. "I haven't had a date since. I keep on friendly but distant terms with the men in my life." Her gaze shifted from his eyes to where her hand lay on his chest. "Until you." She looked up again. "Now...dear Lord, I've cursed you."

He kissed her forehead and pulled her into his arms. "You aren't cursed and nothing's going to happen to me just because we made love tonight."

Grace rested her cheek against his chest, her head moving back and forth. "I shouldn't have risked it. You've been good to me, rescuing me when I was thrown from my horse. This is no way to repay you."

"I didn't ask for payment. I made love to you because I find you intelligent, sexy and brave."

"Not brave," she said, burying her face against his chest. "I ran when Mr. Khalig was killed."

"You had no choice."

"I did. I chose to run."

"You chose to live." He pressed a kiss to her forehead. "Sleep. Tomorrow is another day."

"Tomorrow's another day," she echoed. Her hand slid down his chest to touch him there. "But there's still tonight."

And just like that, he was ready. He jumped out of the bed, ran to where he'd left his wallet in the hallway and returned with protection for round two.

Later, while Grace slept, he slipped from the bed and used the phone in the hallway to call Kevin before midnight. He filled him in on the bullets fired at Grace in his truck. "We will make a full report to the sheriff in the morning. Did the coroner get a positive ID on the body?"

"Yes. It was RJ Khalig."

Caveman's chest tightened. "I should have gotten there sooner."

"How could you have?" Kevin asked. "You didn't know where 'there' was."

His head told him the same, but the man was his assignment and he'd let him down. "Anything on his cause of death?"

"He definitely had a gunshot wound to the chest. The coroner is still trying to determine whether or not it was enough to kill him, and whether he was alive or dead when he fell over the cliff."

Caveman walked into Grace's living room and nudged the curtain aside to look out at the street in front of her house. "My bet is that he was dead. Whoever shot him went back to finish the job." Moonlight shone down on the grass, the driveway and the street. Nothing moved. No vehicles passed.

"We'll know when the coroner's report is complete. In the meantime, how's Ms. Saunders?"

His pulse leaped and his groin tightened. Ms. Saunders was amazing. "Holding her own, but scared."

"She has every right to be." Kevin said something, but the sound was muffled. "I need to go. My wife is getting jealous of my job."

"Sorry to call so late."

"Don't be. I'm here for you. It's like I told you in the beginning, there's a lot more going on than meets the eye. I have a feeling this area is a powder keg waiting for someone to light the fuse."

As much as he would like to disagree with his new boss, he couldn't. In his gut, he knew the man was right.

"Stop by the loft in the morning," Kevin

said. "Maybe Hack will have something on the men who were arguing in the tavern earlier."

"Will do." Caveman ended the call.

A sound drew his attention from the scene through the front window to the woman standing in the doorway to the living room. She stood in the meager light from the moon edging its way around the curtains. Her sandy-blond hair tumbled around her shoulders, her lips were swollen from his kisses and she'd loosely wrapped the sheet from the bed around her naked body.

"For someone who wasn't sure she wanted to make love, you're sending all the wrong signals." He chuckled and stalked toward her, his eyes narrowing as he got closer.

"I woke up, and you were gone."

"Not far. I couldn't leave, knowing there was a beautiful woman keeping the sheets warm."

"The sheets are cold." She lifted her arms to wrap around his neck. As she did, the sheet drifted down past her hips and floated to pool at her ankles.

"Mmm. Perhaps I need to warm them again." He bent, scooped her up into his arms and carried her back to the bedroom. "I'm out of condoms," he said, as he laid her out on the bed and climbed in beside her.

"We'll make do." She touched his cheek. "I just hope that since you're not going to be around for longer than this assignment lasts, you will be immune to the curse."

He turned his face into her hand and kissed her palm. "You're not cursed. And what if I stick around longer?" Now that he was in Wyoming, and the trouble Kevin had mentioned was turning out to be very real and imminent, he didn't see a pressing need for him to return to his unit, just to be sidelined until his leg was 100 percent and he could pass a fitness test. He could stay in Grizzly Pass and get to know Grace a little better, make love to her again…and again.

"Seriously." She brushed her lips across his. "Promise me that you won't fall in love with me. Not that you are or anything. But just to be safe, please…promise me."

His heart twisted. Promise not to love her? Hell, he'd only just met her. How could he fall in love with her so quickly? He kissed her palm again. "Don't you think it's a little early to think about love?" He pressed his lips to the tip of her nose. "Lust, I can understand—"

She touched a finger to his lips. "Please. Just promise."

Caveman opened his mouth to comply, but the words lodged in his throat. "I—" The words she wanted to hear refused to leave his lips. He couldn't even think them. Not love Grace? His twisting heart seemed to open into a gaping void at the thought of leaving Grizzly Pass and never talking to her again. He looked around the room, searching for the right words, knowing there weren't any. His gaze paused at the window. Light shone around the edges of the curtain, a bright white light getting lighter by the moment. He shot a glance at the clock on the nightstand. Was it already morning?

The green numbers on the digital clock read 12:36.

His pulse leaped, he grabbed Grace and rolled to the far side of the bed and off, taking her with him. Just as they landed hard on the floor, a loud crashing sound filled the air, the bed slid toward them, and the mattress upended and slammed them against the wall. Drywall crumbled, sending the ceiling and loose insulation cascading down around them, filling the air with dust so thick Caveman wouldn't have been able to see his hand in front of his face. If he could get his hand free to raise to his face. He and Grace were trapped between the mattress and the wall, unable to move.

Chapter Ten

Grace struggled to turn her head to the side, pulled her face out of a pillow and gasped for air. Something heavy lay on top of her and the mattress held her tightly against the wall. "Caveman?"

He coughed, making his body wiggle against hers, explaining the weight lying across her. "Grace? Are you all right?"

"I think so," she said. "But it's hard to breathe."

An engine sounded really close and the smell of exhaust warred with the dust filling her lungs. "What happened?" she whispered, barely able to draw in enough air to activate her vocal cords.

"I think someone crashed into your house."

"Dear God. How?" She tried to draw in a

deep breath, but with everything smashing her to the floor and wall, she couldn't. The darkness surrounding her was nothing compared to the dizzying fog of losing consciousness. If they didn't get out of there soon, she'd suffocate.

"I...can't...get up." Caveman twisted his shoulders, his hands pressing down on her, searching for something else to brace against and finding nothing.

"Just push against me," she said.

"I'm sorry." He braced a hand on her chest and shoved himself backward, sliding down her body, inch by inch. As he moved past her chest, she was able to get a little more air to her lungs. She dragged it in, uncaring that it was filled with dust. The oxygen cleared her brain.

"I'm out," Caveman said.

She heard the sound of boards being kicked to the side. Then she heard the engine revving and the metal clank of gears shifting; the pressure eased off the mattress and her.

She lay for a moment, letting air fill her lungs. Then she struggled to push the heavy mattress off her.

Suddenly the bed shifted and fell away from her.

Caveman leaned down, extending a hand.

Grace took it and let him draw her to her feet and into his arms.

He held her for a long time, smoothing his hand over her hair. Finally, he pushed her to arm's length and swept his gaze over the length of her. "Are you all right? No broken bones, concussion, abrasions?"

She shook her head and stared around at the disaster that was her bedroom. "Maybe a bruised tailbone, but nothing compared to what it could have been if you hadn't thought so quickly." The front wall was caved in, the ceiling joists lay on the floor, electrical wires sparked dangerously close.

"Where's your breaker box?" Caveman asked.

"In the kitchen."

He scooped her up into his arms and waded through the splintered two-by-fours and broken sheets of drywall until he reached the intact hallway. There, he set her on her feet, grabbed her hand and led the way to the kitchen.

Grace took him to the breaker box in the pantry.

He flipped the master switch, shutting off all electricity to the house. "Gas?"

"Propane tank out back."

Caveman hurried to the front hallway and returned a minute later wearing his jeans. He handed her the clothes she'd shed earlier, her boots and her purse. "Put these on and stand out on the porch while I shut off the gas to the house."

Grace dressed on the back porch, shivering in the cold.

Caveman returned and put his arm around her.

"What happened?" she asked, trembling uncontrollably.

"Someone drove my truck into the house."

"Oh, no. Did it ruin your truck?"

Caveman chuckled. "You were almost killed and you're worried about my truck? Sweetheart, you have to get your priorities straight."

"You were in the same place I was. Which means you were almost killed, as well." She leaned into him, slipping her arm around his waist. "If you hadn't noticed the lights headed our way…"

"Sorry about the rough landing, but at least we're alive."

"The driver?" she asked.

"Took off. I'm sure he's long gone by now."

With his arm still around her, he led her down the back porch stairs and away from the damaged house. "We can't stay here tonight."

"We could go to my folks' place. I have a key." Grace laughed, the sound more like a sob. "If you want to dig it out. It's somewhere in my jewelry box on my dresser…"

"Beneath all the rubble." Caveman shook his head. "Hopefully Kevin can help us out."

"I can't believe someone drove your truck into my house." She turned back. "I can't leave it like this. What if it rains?"

Caveman stared up at the clear night sky. "It's not supposed to rain for a couple days. We can come back in the morning and see what we can salvage." He steered her toward the front of the house where his truck stood, the front end smashed in, one of the tires flat. "We'll have to take your vehicle, unless you want to wait while I attempt to change that flat."

"We'll take my SUV." Grace fished in her purse, pulling out her keys. She handed them to Caveman. "I'd drive, but I'm not feeling very steady right now."

"Don't worry. I'll get us there."

Sitting in the passenger seat of her SUV didn't make her feel any better. Nothing about what had happened in the last thirty-six hours felt right.

Except making love to Caveman. And he wasn't much more than a stranger. A stranger who'd saved her life three times now. That had to make up for the fact that they'd known each other such a short amount of time.

"I think it's time to wake the sheriff." Caveman turned the key in the ignition.

It clicked once, but the engine didn't turn over.

Caveman's hand froze on the key, his brows descending. "Grace, get out."

"But we can't take your truck. It's damaged."

"Just get out. Now!" He reached across the seat, pulled the handle on her door and shoved her through. "Run!"

The pure desperation in his tone shook Grace out of the stunned state she'd been in since her world had come crashing down around her. Her feet grew wings and she ran faster than she had since the high school track team. She didn't know where she was going, as long as it was away from the vehicle.

Twenty feet from her old but trusted SUV, the world exploded around her for the second time that night. She flew forward, landing hard on the ground, the air forced from her lungs, her ears ringing.

She lay for a moment, trying to remember how to breathe.

"Caveman," she said and pushed up to her knees. "Caveman!" she shouted, but couldn't hear an answering response due to the loud ringing in her ears. She ran back to the burning hulk that had been her SUV. He'd been so adamant about getting her out of the vehicle he hadn't had time to get himself out.

Grace reached for the door handle of the burning vehicle. She couldn't leave him in there, she had to get him out. The heat made her skin hurt. Right before her hand touched the metal handle, a voice shouted.

"Grace!"

The sound came to her through her throbbing ears and over the roar of the fire. She turned toward it.

Caveman rounded the edge of the blaze and ran toward her. He pulled her away from the flames and held her close.

Several minutes passed, neither one of them in a hurry to move away.

A siren sounded in the distance and then another. Soon the yard was filled with emergency vehicles. The sheriff's deputy was first on the scene, followed by all of the vehicles belonging to the Grizzly Pass Volunteer Fire Department.

The Emergency Medical Technicians checked Grace and Caveman. Other than a few scrapes and bruises they'd live to see another day.

Soon the blaze was out.

Grace checked on her horse in the pasture on the other side of the barn. The fire had been in the front yard. The barn had sustained no damage, but her horse galloped around the paddock, frightened by the sirens and the smoke.

Caveman helped her catch the horse and soothe him. When she finally released him, he ran to the farthest point away from the smoke.

Grace made certain he had sufficient water before she returned to the front of the house. She and Caveman gave a detailed description of the bullets fired on their way home, and what had happened to her house and finally her vehicle. Caveman borrowed a cell phone from the deputy and placed a call to Kevin. The DHS agent offered to let them sleep in the loft above the tavern until they could come up with another arrangement.

The sheriff appeared shortly after they'd

finished their account. He wore jeans and a denim jacket and looked like he'd just gotten out of bed.

Grace and Caveman recounted their story again for the sheriff's benefit.

"Grace, the man who killed Mr. Khalig is definitely after you. Do you know where you're going from here?"

"The Blue Moose Tavern."

The sheriff frowned. "They're closed."

"We'll be staying in the apartment above the tavern tonight," Caveman said.

"Come. You can ride with me," the sheriff said.

"Please." Grace didn't care who she rode with as long as there was a shower and a clean bed wherever they landed. Grace climbed into the back of the sheriff's vehicle. Caveman slid in next to her and pulled her into the crook of his arm. He was covered in dust and soot, but she didn't care. She was equally dirty, but alive. She nestled against him, but when she closed her eyes, images of the fire burned through her eyelids. Her pulse quickened and her heart thudded against her ribs.

"It's okay. We're going to be okay," Caveman said in that same tone he'd used on her horse. It worked on humans just as well.

Grace felt the tension ease. "I thought you were still in my SUV."

"I got out right after you." He smoothed his hand over her hair. "What's important is that we're both okay."

"I have my men watching the roads leading into and out of town," the sheriff said. "If someone is still out and about, they'll bring him in for questioning."

"Whoever did this will be long gone, if he's smart," Caveman said.

The sheriff glanced at them in his rearview mirror. "Whoever it was is getting more serious about these attacks."

"The question is why?" Grace said. "I couldn't see him from the distance when he killed Mr. Khalig. He should know by now."

"No search warrants have been issued," the sheriff said. "I haven't called anyone in for questioning. He's in the clear. As far as we know, it could have been anyone."

"What good does it do to kill me?" Grace shivered. "I'm nobody. Just a biologist."

Caveman tightened his arm around her.

"Who happened to be in the wrong place at the wrong time and witnessed a murder."

"And escaped before the shooter could kill you, too." Sheriff Scott glanced back at her in the rearview mirror. "You're the one who got away."

Another tremor shook Grace's body. "I can't keep running."

"You can't get out in the open and give him something to shoot at." Caveman held her close. "I won't let you."

"I won't stand by and let him get away with destroying my home, my car and my life."

Caveman frowned. "What do you propose to do?"

She shook her head. "I don't know, but I'll think of something." Snuggling closer, she laid her cheek on his chest. "After a shower and some sleep."

THE LOFT ABOVE the Blue Moose Tavern was a fully furnished apartment with a single bedroom, bathroom and a living room with a foldout couch. The living area had been transformed into an operations center with a bay of computers and a large folding table covered with contour maps.

Kevin and Hack, his computer guru, waited in front of the tavern when the sheriff dropped off Caveman and Grace. The two DHS employees led the tired pair up the stairs. After a quick debriefing, Kevin offered Grace clothes his wife had sent and sweats and a T-shirt for Caveman. "We'll help you sift through the debris at your house tomorrow. For tonight, we hope this will do." Kevin's wife had also sent along a toiletries kit with a tube of toothpaste, shampoo, soap and toothbrushes still in their packages.

Grace gathered the kit, the clothes and a fresh towel. "This is one of those times when I'll gladly claim the 'ladies first' clause." She disappeared into the bathroom leaving the men to discuss the events of the day.

"I don't like it," Caveman said as soon as Grace was out of earshot.

"I don't blame you," Kevin agreed.

"There have been too many near misses today and we have yet to identify who's doing it."

"Do you think maybe there's more than one person involved?" Kevin asked.

"I don't know. But what I do know is that whoever it is knows something about weapons and explosives. He wired Grace's ignition with a damn detonator." Anger bubbled up inside him, spilling over. Caveman stalked away from Hack and Kevin, his fists clenched. He needed to fight back, but he didn't have a clue who he was fighting against. He spun and strode back to where Kevin stood. "If I hadn't gone with my gut when the vehicle didn't start, Grace wouldn't be in this apartment now. If I hadn't been there when she came barreling out of the mountains and was thrown by her horse, she'd be dead."

Kevin nodded. "We're still trying to trace the crates we found in the abandoned mine. Someone did a good job transporting them so that no one could identify their origin. We did a count, though, and based on the empty boxes, there were one hundred AR-15s in those crates. You don't hide one hundred AR-15s just anywhere. Someone has an armory around here and they're stockpiling weapons and ammunition."

"And the infrared satellite images we had from a week ago indicated fifteen individuals who helped unload those weapons. The Vanders family would account for at least four of those heat signatures, which leaves eleven."

"Hell, that's half the people in this county," Caveman said.

"I know this town is small, but there are a lot of outlying homes and ranches comprising the entire community of Grizzly Pass." Kevin scrubbed his hand down his face. The shadows under his eyes made him appear much older. "People are preparing for something. It's our jobs to stop them before they hurt others."

Caveman paced the room again, thinking. "This Free America group. Who are the members?"

"We don't know for certain," Hack said. "LeRoy Vanders and his sons admit to being members. They're talking about who else."

"What about the loudmouth last night in the tavern? Ernie Martin," Caveman shot out.

Kevin nodded. "He's one we're watching."

"I've tapped into his home internet account and his cell phone." Hack pulled out his chair and sat at the bank of computers, bringing up a screen. "His computer is clean, and I'm not finding any significant connections on the cell numbers he calls. If he's communicating with the group, he's doing it in person or on a burner phone I can't trace." He tapped several keys, booting the computer to life.

"You don't have to stay and work through the night," Caveman said. "I'm with Grace. All I want right now is a shower and some sleep."

"Do you want one of us to stand guard while you get some rest?" Kevin asked.

"No." Caveman wanted to be alone. With Grace. "The sheriff will have a deputy swing by every half hour until daylight. We should be all right."

Kevin straightened. "Then we'll leave you to get some rest. The sofa folds out into a queen-size bed. You can find sheets and blankets in the chest at the end of the bed. Help yourselves to anything in the refrigerator. I had it stocked with drinks and snacks."

"Thanks." Caveman could hear the shower going in the other room.

Hack powered the computer off and followed Kevin to the door.

"If you need me, give me a call. I can be here in five minutes." Kevin held out his hand. "Bet you weren't counting on so much activity in Wyoming. Were you?"

Caveman shook the man's hand. "No, I thought this would be a mini vacation and I'd be on my way back to my unit."

"And now?"

"I'm beginning to understand your concerns." And he couldn't leave, knowing Grace was in trouble.

"So you'll stay a little longer?"

"As long as you need me and my unit doesn't."

Kevin nodded. "Glad to hear it. We need good soldiers like you."

"I'll do what I can."

"I'm only five minutes away, as well," Hack said. He held up his cell phone. "Call, if you need me."

"Roger." Caveman closed the door behind the two men and twisted the dead bolt lock. Not that a dead bolt would have stopped a truck from crashing through Grace's bedroom wall. He hurried to the back of the apartment, stripping off his dirty clothes and kicking off his boots. The shower was still going when he stepped through the bathroom door.

He pushed the curtain aside and slipped into the tub.

"I wondered how long it would take you to get rid of those two." Grace turned around, her body clean and glistening beneath the spray. "I was beginning to prune." She slid a handful of suds over his chest, making mud out of the dirt, soot and dust.

Caveman didn't care. She could smear mud all over his body if she wanted as long as her hands were doing the smearing. She poured shampoo into her palm and lathered his hair.

With his hands free to explore, he lathered up and smoothed his fingers over her shoulders and down to her breasts, where he tweaked the nipples into tight buds. Moving lower, he cupped her sex and parted her folds, strumming the nubbin of flesh between.

She moaned and widened her stance. "No protection," she said, her voice catching in her throat as he flicked her there again.

"This isn't about me."

Grace moaned again, her hand sliding over his shoulders, washing away all of the grime, dirty bubbles carrying it down the drain. "Not all about me." She wrapped her hands around his shaft and stroked the length of him.

It was his turn to groan.

Touching and testing the sweet spots, they felt their way to an orgasm that left Caveman satisfied and frustrated at the same time. First thing in the morning, he'd hit the local drug store for reinforcements. This woman's appetite rivaled his own, and he didn't want to be caught unprepared.

By the time they'd explored every inch of each other's body, the water had cooled to the point of discomfort.

Caveman turned off the shower, grabbed a towel and gently dried Grace. She returned the favor and sighed, her face sad.

"Why so sad?" he asked. "Didn't you like that?"

"Too much." She took his hand and led him to the bed. "I'm going to miss it when you're gone."

"Who said I'm going anywhere?"

"You know what I mean." She lay down on the bed and scooted over, making room for him. "You said it yourself. You're only going to be here for a short time."

"What if I decide to stay?" He might not have a job to go back to in the army. If the Medical Review Board didn't clear him, he'd be discharged, or given a desk job. He'd rather move back to Montana or Wyoming than take a desk job.

Grace's brows descended. "You can't stay. Look what nearly happened tonight. You were almost killed."

"But I wasn't. And neither were you."

She snuggled closer, her eyes drooping. "I'm too tired to argue about it. Just keep your promise, and don't do something stupid like fall in love with me." Her voice trailed off and her breathing grew steadier.

Caveman brushed a strand of hair away from her cheek and bent to kiss her. "I never made that promise. And it might be too late." Never in a million years, would Max "Caveman" Decker have guessed he would fall in love with a woman after knowing her for less than a week. But the thought of leaving and going back to his unit didn't hold the same appeal. In fact, even the mention of leaving made him feel like someone had a hand on his heart, squeezing the life out of him.

Maybe it was too soon for love, but only time would tell. Caveman wasn't so sure he'd have the time to find out, if Khalig's killer had his way with Grace. Tonight would have been the end of her had Caveman left when he'd originally wanted. Now, he couldn't leave. Not as long as Grace was in danger.

Chapter Eleven

Grace slept until after ten the following morning. When she woke, she stretched her arm across the bed, expecting to feel a naked body next to hers. When she didn't, she opened her eyes.

Caveman was gone.

For a moment, panic ripped through her. After all that had happened, she'd begun to rely on him to rescue her. Then she reminded herself he wouldn't have left without saying goodbye. Not after last night.

They'd shared more than a near-death experience, they'd connected on a level even more intimate.

Male voices sounded through the paneling of the bedroom door.

Grace bolted to a sitting position, dragging

the sheet up over her bare breasts. She'd forgotten that the living area was being used as the command center for the DHS representatives. They'd probably been there for at least an hour, while she'd slept in.

Her cheeks heated. She wondered if Caveman had risen before they arrived to spare her the embarrassment of the team finding them in bed together.

She rose, grabbed the clothes Kevin's wife had provided and slipped into the bathroom. Five minutes later, she was dressed, had her hair pulled back into a neat ponytail and had brushed her teeth. She was ready to face the world. Or at least Kevin's team. She opened the door to the bedroom and stepped out.

The group of men standing around the array of computer monitors turned as one.

Heat rose into Grace's cheeks. Did they know she and Caveman had slept naked in the next room? Did she care? She squared her shoulders and forced a smile to her face.

In addition to Kevin, Caveman and Hack, three more men were in attendance. All there to witness Grace emerging from the back bedroom. Yeah, not what a woman wanted that early in the morning. "Good morning."

"Grace." Kevin stepped forward. "I trust you slept well?"

She nodded, her gaze going to the three men she didn't recognize.

Kevin turned to them. "Grace, have you met the other members of my task force?"

"No, I have not."

He turned to a big man with red hair and blue eyes. "This is Jon Caspar, US Navy SEAL. They call him Ghost."

Ghost shook her hand. "I've seen you around. Nice to meet you."

Kevin moved to the next man, who was not quite as tall as Ghost, but had black hair and ice-blue eyes. "Trace Walsh, aka Hawkeye, is an Army Ranger."

Grace shook hands with Hawkeye. "Pleasure to meet you."

He grinned. "The pleasure's all mine."

Caveman grunted behind her. If she wasn't mistaken, it was a grunt of anger, maybe jealousy? Her heart swelled.

The last man Kevin introduced had really short auburn hair and hazel eyes. Almost as tall as Ghost, he looked like he could chew nails and spit them out. "This is Rex Trainor."

"My friends call me T-Rex." The man stuck out a hand. "I'm with the US Marine Corps."

When T-Rex shook her hand, he nearly crushed the bones.

Introductions complete, Grace glanced at the computer monitors. "Am I missing something?"

Kevin shook his head. "Not at all. We were just going through some of the most likely suspects who live in the area."

"Like?" She stepped up beside Caveman and looked over Hack's shoulder at pictures of people on the different monitors. Some of them were mug shots, others were driver's license pictures or photos from yearbooks. She recognized most of them, having lived in the area for the majority of her life. Small-town life was like that.

"Quincy Kemp and Ernie Martin," Caveman said.

"Mathis Herrington, Wayne Batson," Kevin added.

"And, of course, Tim Cramer and the Vanders family, who have already been detained." Hack tapped the keys on the computer keyboard. "We've been trying to find the connection between all of them."

Grace yawned and stretched, her muscles sore from everything that had happened over the past couple of days. "Has anyone thought to ask Mrs. Penders at the grocery store?"

Four of the five men frowned.

Ghost grinned. "That's where my girl, Charlie McClain, goes when she wants to know what's going on. Mrs. Penders seems to have her finger on the pulse of everything going on in town."

"I'll go question her." Caveman turned toward the door. "Mrs. Penders is her name?"

Grace held up her hand. "You can't just barge in and interrogate the woman. She likes to gossip, not answer a barrage of very pointed questions. Since my house was destroyed last night, she'll be eager to hear all of the details straight from the horse's mouth. Give a little, get a lot." She glanced down at the clothes Kevin's wife had loaned her. "Kevin, tell your wife thank you for the loaner. I'll get them back as soon as I dig my wardrobe out from under the rubble."

"She said to keep them as long as you need them," Kevin said. "And we plan to help with the cleanup."

"Thanks, but I'd rather you found the killer."

She drew in a deep breath and let it out. "I don't know how much longer I can play this game with him, before he scores." *With my death.* "Now, if you will excuse me, I'm going across the street to talk to Mrs. Penders and buy a few supplies I might need in the cleanup process."

"I'm going with you," Caveman said.

Grace shook her head. "You can't. Mrs. Penders will be more likely to talk if I'm alone."

"You can't waltz around town like anyone else." Caveman gripped her arms. "You have a killer after you. One who is a crack shot with a rifle and scope."

Placing a hand on his chest, Grace smiled up at him. "Then I'll zigzag, or whatever it is you trained combatants do to run through enemy territory."

The other men chuckled. Not Caveman.

His face hardened. "It's not a joke."

Her smile fading, Grace nodded. "I know. It's not every day you have someone drive a truck into your bedroom, or have someone shooting at you. I'll be careful and look for trouble before I cross the street."

"I'm walking you across the street."

Her first instinct was to argue, but one glance at Caveman's face and she knew she would lose that argument. And frankly, she liked having him around. "Okay." She walked to the door and followed Caveman down the steps to the street.

He looped his arm around her shoulders, pulling her close to his body. They probably appeared to be lovers who couldn't get enough of each other. After last night, the look fit Grace. She wondered if Caveman felt the same, or if he truly only thought of her as a temporary distraction until he returned to his unit.

At the corner of the grocery store, Grace stopped and placed a hand on Caveman's chest. "This is where I get off. I'll see you as soon as I get all of the information I can out of Mrs. Penders."

"I'll be right here. All you have to do is yell if you need me."

"Thank you." Then, before she could talk herself out of it, she leaned up on her toes and pressed her lips to his. It was meant to be a quick show of appreciation. However, she was more than gratified when Caveman took the kiss to the next level.

He cinched his arm around her waist, crushing her to his body, his lips claiming hers in a kiss that stole her breath away and made her knees turn to gelatin. Had Caveman not been holding her, she would have melted to the ground. When he set her away from him, she swayed.

She raised a hand to her lips. "Wow."

He chuckled, the warm, deep resonance of the sound heating her from the inside out. "I don't like you standing out in the open for long." He turned her toward the grocery store entrance, gave her bottom a pat and sent her on her way. "Hurry back. I have more where that came from."

She ran her tongue across her bottom lip, tasting him.

"On second thought, forget going inside. We can drive out to the local lake and make out in the backseat of my pickup."

She laughed. "You're not making this easy."

He held up his hands. "What am I supposed to make easy?"

"Letting go of you when you leave Grizzly Pass."

"Maybe that's my plan."

Her smile faded. "You have to, eventually."

"Let's not talk about that now. In fact, take

your time inside. Don't come out until you see me walk by the windows. I want to look around town."

She snorted. "That won't take long."

"Exactly. So take all the time you need. Just don't come outside until I'm here to protect you."

She nodded. Grace wanted to run for the door, zip in, suck information out of Mrs. Pender's brain in record time and return for another of those soul-defining kisses.

She'd warned him not to fall in love with her, but maybe she'd been warning the wrong person. Grace needed to take her own advice. Perhaps the curse was on anyone *she* fell in love with, not who fell in love with her.

With no time to contemplate her thoughts, she stepped into the store and greeted the female store owner with a smile. "Good morning, Mrs. Penders."

"Grace, honey, I was shocked to hear someone bulldozed your house last night. What can I do to help?"

OUTSIDE, LEANING ON a light post, Caveman studied the people who entered and exited the small store. The only one of its kind in town, it had the corner on the market. If people wanted more than what the Penderses offered, they had to drive thirty minutes to an hour to the nearest big town. Too far for a loaf of bread or a gallon of milk.

After a few minutes, he pushed away from the light post and walked to the end of the block—still within a reasonable distance to listen for a scream or see someone entering the store who might appear to be there for nefarious reasons rather than to buy a can of soup or a loaf of bread.

From his vantage point at the street corner, he could see to the end of Main Street. A storefront on the opposite side had a stuffed bear outside on the sidewalk. Not the teddy bear of the fake fur, cotton-filled variety. No, this was an eleven-foot tall grizzly, professionally mounted by a skillful taxidermist. He stood on his hind legs, his front legs outstretched, the wicked claws appearing to be ready to swipe at passersby. And the mouth was open, every razor-sharp tooth on display. Yes, Quincy Kemp was very good at making the carcasses appear alive.

With a quick glance toward the grocery store to make certain Grace hadn't ended her information-gathering mission early, he turned toward the meat processing and taxidermist shop.

The door stood open; the scents of cedar, pepper and the musk of animal hides filled his senses, bringing back memories of a similar place in Caveman's hometown. In states where hunting was the major pastime of residents and tourists, every town seemed to have one of these kinds of stores.

A man emerged from a back room, wiping his hands on a towel. "What can I do for you?"

Caveman recognized him as Quincy Kemp. "I heard you made jerky."

"You heard right," Quincy said with one of the best poker faces Caveman had encountered.

"Do you happen to have buffalo or venison jerky?"

The man nodded and pulled a plastic butter tub from beneath the counter, opened it and selected a strip of jerky. "Try before you buy. I don't do refunds. This is buffalo."

Caveman popped the piece of jerky in his mouth and then chewed and chewed. The explosion of flavors made his mouth water.

Quincy crossed his arms over his chest,

lifted his chin and looked down his nose at Caveman. "Well?"

"Good. I'd like to purchase a pound of the buffalo jerky."

While Quincy weighed several strips of the flavored, dried meat, Caveman wandered around the store. Besides a glass case of jerky and a refrigerated case of raw meat labeled Beef, Venison, Buffalo, Elk and Red Deer, there were numerous animals mounted on the wall.

"Did you do all of these?" Caveman waved at the lifelike animals staring down at him from shelves and nooks along the wall.

Quincy slipped the strips of jerky into a plastic bag and sealed it before answering. "Yeah. That'll be fifteen bucks."

Caveman fished his wallet out of his pocket, which reminded him he needed to hit the store for a refill of condoms. He placed a twenty on the counter. "What kinds of animals have you done?"

"What you see."

Caveman had noticed the bear, bobcat, rattle snake, elk, moose and coyote. "What about mountain lion?"

"I've done a couple."

"Bobcat?"

He shrugged. "Four."

"Is there an open season on bobcat and mountain lion?"

The man's eyes narrowed. "Do you have a point?"

"Just wondering. I might like to buy a hunting license while I'm here."

Quincy slapped the change on the counter and pushed the plastic bag of jerky toward Caveman. "Hunting season isn't open until the fall. If that's all you want, I don't have time to talk. I have work to do."

Caveman lifted the bag of jerky and grinned. "Thanks."

Quincy didn't wait for Caveman to leave the store before he returned to the back room.

Caveman would like to have followed the man to the back to see what job he was all fired up about. The man looked like someone who could chew nails. Not that he scared Caveman, but he wouldn't take kindly to being followed.

But then, Caveman could claim he wanted to see Quincy's work in case he wanted the man to stuff his next trophy kill. Not that Caveman ever killed just for the trophy. He hunted back in Montana, but always ate what he bagged.

Easing behind the counter, Caveman worked his way to the door leading to the back of the building. Quincy had left it open, presumably to hear for customers entering the shop.

Through the door was a workroom filled with hides and tools of the taxidermist trade. A short corridor led to a workshop in the back. The meat packaging plant was probably at the end of the hallway.

Quincy was nowhere to be seen.

Caveman studied the hides, curious about what the taxidermist did.

"Hey!" Quincy emerged from a door in the back. "What are you doing back here?"

Startled by the man's abrupt appearance, Caveman snapped around, his legs bent in a ready stance, his fists clenched in a defensive reflex. "I had a question for you."

"Well, take it out to the front. Nobody comes back here, but me."

"Sorry." Caveman held up his hands in surrender. "I didn't touch anything."

"Doesn't matter. You don't belong back here." Quincy marched toward him.

Caveman backed through the door, pretending to be afraid, but ready to take on the man if he pushed him too far. "I wanted to know if you could stuff a wolf I hit on my way into town. I threw him in the back of my truck, hating to waste a good-looking hide. I think he'd look really great in my man cave back home in North Carolina."

"Man, you need to get rid of the carcass. It's illegal to keep a wolf, dead or alive, in the state of Wyoming."

"So you wouldn't stuff him? What if I sneak him in here at night? Could you?"

"Hell, no. I don't plan on spending the next five years in jail. Been there, done that. I'm never going back. I'd die before I let them take me back."

"Okay. I totally understand. No worries. I'll find someone else to do it."

"You won't."

"Won't what?"

"Find another taxidermist. No one will touch a wolf, unless the government commissions it."

"Well, there goes my idea for a centerpiece in my living room." Caveman raised a hand in a half wave. "I guess that's all I needed to know. I must say, I'm disappointed."

Quincy's mouth formed into a tightly pressed line and his eyes narrowed.

Caveman waved the bag of jerky again.

"Thanks again for the jerky and all the information on taxidermist rules in Wyoming." He left the shop and strolled down the street toward the tavern, his gaze on the grocery store where he'd left Grace.

When he was far enough away from Quincy's shop, Caveman crossed the street and waited outside the grocery store, chewing on the buffalo jerky he'd purchased from Quincy, wondering what the man might be hiding in the back of his building. Perhaps he'd bring it up to Kevin and let the boss decide who he could send in to check. At this point, from what Caveman could tell of his role with Task Force Safe Haven, his primary purpose was to protect Grace from a killer. Kevin and the others could do the sleuthing to find out if what was happening in Grizzly Pass was a terrorist plot to take over the government.

"MARK RUTHERFORD SHOULD be available to help you fix the damage to your house. He's a good handyman and carpenter. And Lord knows he could use the work," Mrs. Penders said. "What with his daddy having to pay the additional grazing fees when he just forked out a wad of cash to install a new pump in his well. I'm sure Mark would appreciate the extra income."

"I'll check with him as soon as I assess the damage. I just can't understand why someone would deliberately crash into my house."

"Are you sure it wasn't an accident?"

"No, it was deliberate. He broke into the truck and drove it into my bedroom wall as if he knew I was in bed." Grace glanced around the store. "I'll need some trash bags and cleaning supplies."

"Sweetie, let me help you."

"Oh, I can't take you away from the register."

"There's no one in the store right now. I want to help." Mrs. Penders locked the register and led the way down the aisle of cleaning supplies, plucking off a couple bottles of disinfectant spray and cleaner. "I don't know what's going on in town, what with the Vanderses going crazy and kidnapping a busload of little ones. And now someone's murdered Mr. Khalig. He came into the store the other day for a bag of butterscotch candies." She smiled sadly. "Such a nice man. I imagine his wife will be devastated."

"Who would want to kill Mr. Khalig?"

Mrs. Penders rounded the end of the cleaning supplies aisle and started up the one with paper products and boxes of trash bags. She grabbed one of the boxes, read the front and put it back, selecting one with a larger number of bags. "Mr. Khalig worked as an inspector for the pipeline. If he doesn't approve what's going on, the pipeline shuts down. He could have reported some safety issues. Some people think he's the reason they got laid off."

"Did he ever say anything about any safety issues?" Grace asked, taking some of the cleaning supplies from Mrs. Penders. They walked back to front of the store and set the items on the counter.

"I could use some paper plates and disposable cutlery. I have a feeling my electricity will be off and on as they work on my house."

Mrs. Penders turned and led the way to the plastic forks and spoons. "Mr. Khalig wasn't allowed to discuss his work on account of confidentiality. But I could tell he wasn't happy with what he was finding. He started out warm and friendly. The longer he was here, the quieter and more secretive he became. And he kept looking over his shoulder, like someone was watching him." Mrs. Penders sighed. "And somebody had to have been, in order to shoot him from a distance. Poor, poor man. How awful."

"How do you know all of this?"

Mrs. Penders carried the boxes of spoons and forks to the counter and gave Grace a smile. "I just do. As for who, there are quite a few people I can think of. All of them worked for the pipeline and lost their jobs. The sheriff should start there. I mean look at what happened with Tim Cramer. He lost his job with the pipeline, his wife filed for divorce and now he's in jail. He was so desperate he helped with that kidnapping."

"He couldn't have been the one to kill Mr. Khalig. He was in jail when it happened."

"True. But there are others on the verge of bankruptcy, losing their homes and destroying their families." Mrs. Penders clucked her tongue. "Such a shame. I wish that pipeline had never crossed this state."

"Most of those who worked for the pipeline would have moved out of state to find jobs by now."

"Yes, but they wouldn't be as desperate." Mrs. Penders unlocked the register. "It's as if someone is sabotaging this area and the people in it."

"Who would do that, and why?" As Mrs. Penders rang up Grace's purchases, Grace put them into a bag. "We don't have anything here anyone would want."

"Maybe they want the pipeline to fail, but then maybe not, if they shot the inspector who could have shut down the whole thing." Mrs. Penders took Grace's money and handed her the change. "Then there are the folks who are tired of everything to do with the government. They would prefer to have the entire state of Wyoming secede from the United States. Bunch of crazies, if you ask me. Even scarier, they're a bunch of armed nut jobs."

"Do you know any of them?"

"Nobody comes out and says they're part of the group Free America. But I have my suspicions."

"Who?"

The older woman glanced around to make sure no one else was in the store. "I think Ernie Martin, Quincy Kemp, Don Sweeney and Mathis Herrington belong to that group. I'm sure there are a lot more who aren't as vocal. Some not from this county, but a county over."

"If they aren't telling you, how do you know?"

The older woman lifted her chin. "I have ears. Sometimes they run into each other in the store while I'm stocking shelves. I can hear them talking. In fact, I'm pretty sure they're having some meeting tomorrow night."

Butterflies erupted in Grace's belly. "Where?"

Mrs. Penders shrugged. "I don't know. Ernie and Quincy were in here buying lighter fluid and briquettes earlier today for a barbeque. They said something about getting together at the range."

"Range?" Grace's mind exploded with possibilities. "As in front range? Good Lord, that could be almost anywhere." Or maybe… "Or do they mean like a gun range?"

A mother carrying a baby in a car seat walked into the store.

The store owner smiled at the woman. "Good morning, Bayleigh, how's Lucas?"

The young mother smiled. "He's finally sleeping through the night."

"That's wonderful. Are you here for that formula you ordered?"

"I am," Bayleigh answered.

Mrs. Penders raised her finger. "One minute. I'll get it from the back."

"Please, take your time," Bayleigh said. "I have other shopping to do."

Grace gathered her bags. She couldn't take up any more of Mrs. Penders's time. "Thank you for everything, Mrs. P."

"Let me know if you need anything. Remember to check with Mark Rutherford. He's got time on his hands and probably can start right away on the repairs."

"I'll do that." Grace paused at the entrance, a frown pulling at her brows. A meeting at the range. When she spotted Caveman waiting outside, she pushed through the door and hurried toward the man who made her heart beat faster. "We need to talk to the team."

Chapter Twelve

Caveman paced the length of the operations center.

"How do you propose we get an invite to that meeting tomorrow evening?" Kevin asked. "We're not even sure what Mrs. Penders meant by 'the range.'"

"I'd bet my last dollar it's Wayne Batson's gun range," Ghost said.

Hack nodded. "He has the fences and security system in place to hold off an initial attack. And his computer system has a helluva firewall. I've yet to hack into it."

"Sounds like someone with something to hide," Caveman said.

"Why don't we just walk in?" Grace asked.

All five men turned toward her.

"Walk in?" Kevin asked. "What do you mean?"

"By now, everyone in town will know I've been the target of a shooter and someone who likes crashing trucks into my house. What if I ask Wayne to give me some time on his range, maybe even shooting lessons?"

"No way," Caveman said. "Putting you on a rifle range with a bunch of loaded weapons is a recipe for getting shot. What if the shooter is Wayne or one of his buddies?"

"So, I take my bodyguard and announce it to the world I'm going to the range. The sheriff knows, everyone in town knows. If someone shoots me at the range, they'll have to shoot Caveman, too. They might get away with an accident killing one person, but they won't get away with killing two."

Anger tinged with a healthy dose of fear bubbled up inside Caveman. "So who shall we offer up as the one?" He shook his head. "It's too dangerous."

Grace turned toward Kevin. "At the very least, we go in, find the weaknesses of Batson's security system, leave and come back at night when we can slip in under the cover of darkness."

Caveman couldn't believe what she was saying. If one of Batson's friends was the shooter, he'd have no trouble lining up his sights and taking her down. "There is no 'we' in slipping back into Batson's property." He poked a finger at her. "*You're* not going anywhere."

"But I'm the one with the big target on my back."

Crossing his arms over his chest, he refused to back down. "Exactly. Now you're beginning to understand."

Her frown deepened and her cheeks reddened. "Don't patronize me, Max Decker. I'm the one who has to keep looking over her shoulder. I'm the one whose house is now a wreck. I have the biggest stake in finding the killer. I deserve to go."

"But you don't deserve to die." His face firmed and his eyes narrowed. "You're not going."

Her chin lifted. "Then I'll go without you. I need practice with my .40-caliber pistol, and I don't need your permission." She started for the door. "Gentlemen, I have a house to sift through and arrangements to make to get me onto Batson's rifle range." She sailed past Caveman and almost made it to the door when he grabbed her arm and yanked her back.

"We need to talk," he said. He couldn't let

her walk out the door unprotected and waltz into the enemy's camp. If Batson was truly the enemy. "Let's at least talk this through before we go off half-cocked."

"I'm done talking." She glared at the hand on her arm. "Let go of me."

"Grace." Kevin stepped over to where they stood by the door. "We need to make a plan. We also need to understand who we're dealing with. What motivation does Wayne Batson have to host a Free America meeting on his range?"

"Maybe he's training recruits for the take-over of the government," Ghost offered. "The message Charlie picked up off that social media site was clear. They're planning a take-over of something."

"Why would Batson lead the charge?" Kevin asked. "He has to have a reason."

Grace pressed her fingers to the bridge of her nose. "I don't know. Wayne Batson seems to be the only person in the county who has pulled himself up out of hard times. When he was faced with bankruptcy, he found inves-tors and turned his ranch into a sportsman's paradise. Why destroy a good thing by plot-ting against the government?"

"Having been in a bad situation, maybe he harbors animosity toward the government for some reason," Hawkeye said. "You never know what will push a man over the edge and make him think he has to take control of the world."

"Are you saying we might be barking up the wrong tree?" Grace asked. "That Batson might not be our guy? His ranch with the rifle range might not be the meeting place?"

Kevin shook his head. "No. I think you're on to something."

"Then what's your plan?" She planted her fists on her hips. "If I take Caveman with me to practice my shooting skills, we can at least get inside and look around."

Caveman turned toward Kevin. "What do you have in the way of communications equipment? We had the radio headsets we used when we stormed the Lucky Lou Mine in the rescue attempt to save the kidnapped kids. Could we have something like that? And do you have any kind of webcam we can hide in a pen?"

Kevin grinned. "You must have me mistaken with the CIA."

Hack spun in his chair and opened his mouth to say something.

Before he could, Kevin held up his hand. "As

a matter of fact, I invested some of the project funding in just what you're talking about. We have a webcam button we can attach to your shirt. Hack will get you two wired up."

Grace smiled. "Thank you."

Caveman wasn't happy about the situation, but he could either shut up and go, or send someone else with Grace. The woman was going whether or not he wanted her to. And because he found himself just a little bit protective of her, he didn't trust anyone else to take care of her as well as he would. Not that the others weren't fully capable. They just didn't have the connection he had with her.

Hack went to a footlocker in the corner, unlocked the combination lock and pulled out radio headsets and a small case with a little white button. "Doesn't look like much, but it sends a pretty clear picture to our computer." He handed it to Grace. "The idea is to replace a button on a shirt, so it will take a little bit of sewing skills." He handed her a small sewing kit like the ones found in hotel rooms.

"I can handle that." She glanced at Caveman. "Since your shirt has the buttons and you'll know better what to look for, you should have the camera on you. I can sew this onto your shirt."

"I'm pretty handy with a needle and thread, if you'd rather I did it," he offered.

"No use taking off your shirt. Let me call Batson and see if we can even get onto the range this afternoon."

Hack looked up the Lonesome Pine Ranch and passed her the contact number.

Grace pulled her cell phone from her purse, entered the number and waited.

Part of Caveman wished no one would answer or, if they did, they wouldn't allow her to book time on the gun range.

"This is Grace Saunders. I've had some troubles lately with someone following me."

Caveman snorted softly. Grace had conveniently left off the fact that someone was not only following her, but trying to kill her.

"Thank you. Yes, I'm okay," Grace said. "The sheriff suggested I call and see if I could get some time on the range to practice with my pistol. The sooner the better. I was hoping to get out there this afternoon. It will be two of us. Me and my…boyfriend." She paused, nodding at whatever the person on the other end of the call was telling her. "That would be great. Four o'clock works perfectly. Yes, we'll bring our own guns. I'll see you at four. Thank you." She clicked the end call button and looked across at Caveman. "We're on for four o'clock. I might have to dig my pistol out from under the rubble of my bedroom."

"I have one you could use," Kevin offered.

"If I can't find mine, I'll take you up on the offer," Grace said. "In the meantime, I'd like to get something going on the cleanup effort at my house. I don't want to wait until it rains and ruins even more of my belongings."

For the next few hours, Grace was on the phone with an insurance adjuster and a handyman.

Caveman took her out to her house to meet with the adjuster. Once the man left with a page full of notes, Caveman started sorting through broken boards and crumbled drywall to get to Grace's nightstand where she kept her pistol. He helped her locate the boxes of bullets she'd need at the range.

They cleared enough debris to allow her to get into her drawers and closets to pack several suitcases. Without a way to lock her home, she couldn't stay in the house until the wall was back up.

Grace called Mark Rutherford, the handyman Mrs. Penders had recommended. He showed up, surveyed the damage and gave her an estimate on how much it would cost to fix it. He'd only take a week to clear the debris and rebuild the wall. He'd need the better part of the next week to do the finishing work on the inside and outside.

Throughout the day, he watched Grace handle the disaster of her house with calm and patience, talking to the handyman and the adjuster with a smile and a handshake. The sheriff came out to survey the damage in the daylight and take pictures of the house and the truck. When she told him she'd be going out to Wayne Batson's range for target practice, he nodded.

"It's a good idea to be proficient and have confidence in the handling of your own weapon."

She didn't tell him why she'd chosen Batson's range or that there might be a meeting of the Free America group there the next night.

Caveman was tempted, but he figured she didn't want the sheriff to try to talk her out of it.

His gut clenched all day. He was torn between calling the whole thing off and going through with the plan. If they could get in and out without being shot and killed, they could bring back enough information for the task force team to enter the secure ranch compound. The team could find out what the rebel group was planning and maybe determine who might have killed Mr. Khalig.

After the sheriff left, Caveman brought a mug of hot cocoa out to the porch for Grace and insisted she sit for a few minutes. She chose the porch swing and sat far enough over for Caveman to join her. "How did you make hot cocoa?"

Caveman grinned. "I found a camp stove in a closet."

For a few minutes, they shared the silence, sipping cocoa and staring at the caved-in portion of her home.

"Why would a rebel group like Free America want to kill a pipeline inspector? They don't work for the government. They contract out to the big oil companies." Grace sighed. "I hope we're not wasting our time going out to the Lonesome Pine Ranch, chasing a wild goose."

"If you're concerned, why don't you stay in town and let me go alone? The activities of the Free America group are a concern of Task Force Safe Haven. Kevin's responsibility as an agent with the Department of Homeland Security is to keep our homeland safe. If this group is planning to take a government facility that would be considered an act of terror. We have to investigate. This is the first real information we've received on when and where they will meet. We have to check it out. But you don't."

"If they have anything to do with Mr. Khalig's death and the subsequent threats to my life, I sure as hell have to go. I refuse to continue playing the victim. It's time I fought back."

Caveman took her empty cup and set it on the end table beside the swing and put his next to it. Then he took Grace's hands in his. "I want you to promise you won't do anything that will make Batson or his employees think we're spying on him. If he is part of this rebel group, he might want to keep it under wraps. In which case, he might go to all lengths to keep that secret."

"I promise I will do my best not to draw unnecessary attention. We'll get in there, and get out with the data your team needs to do what they have to do to protect our nation."

"Then we'd better get going. Your appointment is for four o'clock." He stood, pulled her to her feet and into his arms.

She rested her hands on his chest. "Are you going to kiss me?"

He chuckled. "I'm thinking about it."

Her hands slipped up around his neck. "Stop thinking, and start kissing."

"Do you still think your curse will be the death of me?"

"Not if we don't fall in love."

If her curse was real, he was doomed. In the short amount of time he'd been with Grace, she'd found her way into his mind, body and soul. He knew there would be no going back. Convincing her that she wouldn't kill him with a crazy curse would be the first challenge. Figuring out where they'd go from Grizzly Pass would be the second.

She laced her fingers at the back of his head and pulled his head down to hers. "Now, are you going to kiss me?"

"Damn right, I am." His lips crashed down on hers, his tongue pushing past her teeth to caress hers. This was what he'd wanted all day.

Grace didn't hold back. Her tongue twisted and thrust, her body pressing tightly to his.

When he had to breathe again, Caveman rested his cheek against her temple. "I worry about you," he whispered.

"You don't have to. I can make my own decisions and live with the consequences of my actions."

His chest tightened as if someone was squeezing him really hard. "If you're fortunate enough to live."

GRACE CLENCHED HER hands in her lap, as she stared at the road ahead, with every intention of staying alive. As far as she was concerned, she was going to get in some target practice with her handgun. Then she'd leave. If they just happened to find out more about a certain antigovernment organization, so be it. She'd keep those little gems of information to herself until she was off the Lonesome Pine Ranch and back where it was safe.

She had no problem letting the trained soldiers handle the major spying mission, although she would love to be a fly on the wall and listen in on the Free America meeting. After all, it was her country, too. She didn't appreciate terrorists trying to take over the land of the free and the home of the brave.

But she wasn't trained in combat tactics and would slow them down. She'd help them more by gathering information that would help them infiltrate after dark.

She'd sewn the webcam button onto Caveman's shirt and watched as he tucked the radio communication device in his ear. She put one in hers as well, but she wasn't as confident using it. She turned her head away from Caveman. "Can you hear me?"

"Loud and clear," he said.

"We can hear you, too," Hack said from his desk in the operations center.

Grace grinned. "I feel like I fell into a spy movie."

"Yeah, well, this isn't make-believe. Stick to the script and keep a low profile."

"Got it." Grace's heartbeat sped as Caveman pulled up to the gate of the Lonesome Pine Ranch and punched the button on the control panel.

"Grace Saunders and Max Decker here for range practice," he said into the speaker.

"Welcome. Please drive through." The giant wrought-iron gate swung open.

Caveman pulled through the gate.

Grace glanced over her shoulder as the big

gate closed. Her breath caught in her throat. For a moment, she felt like an animal caught in a trap. Forcing a calm she didn't feel, she smiled over at Caveman. "Ready for some target practice?"

"You bet." He laid his hand over the console.

Grace placed hers in his for a brief squeeze before he returned his grip to the steering wheel.

Signs for the gun range directed them to turn before they reached the big house perched on top of a hill. The road ended in a small parking area. Wayne Batson waited for them, a holster buckled around his hips. In his cowboy boots, jeans and leather vest, he looked like a man straight out of the Old West.

A shiver rippled across Grace's skin. What if this man was the one who'd been shooting at her? Would he take the opportunity now to kill her? Maybe she'd been a little too naive to think a killer wouldn't shoot her in broad daylight even when the sheriff knew where she was going.

Instead of an old-fashioned revolver in the holster, Wayne had a sleek, dark-gray pistol, probably a 9-millimeter by the size and shape.

Grace pasted a smile on her face and climbed

out of the truck. "Good afternoon, Mr. Batson. Thank you for letting me come out for some target practice on such short notice."

"My pleasure," he said. "I hear you're having a little trouble and want to make sure you can defend yourself."

She nodded. "I've had this gun since I graduated from college, but I don't get nearly enough practice with it."

"No use having one if you don't know how to use it properly," Batson said.

"I told her the same." Caveman stepped up to Batson and held out his hand. "Max Decker. You must be Wayne Batson, the owner of Lonesome Pine Ranch?"

Batson nodded and shook his hand. "It's been in the family for over a century. I hope to keep it in the family for another century." He glanced from Caveman to Grace. "Show me what you have in the way of firepower."

Grace pulled out the case with her .40-caliber H&K pistol. It was small, light and fit her hand perfectly.

Caveman brought out a 9-millimeter Glock.

Batson assigned them lanes on the range and handed them paper targets. Once the targets were stapled in place, they stood back at the firing position.

Batson joined Grace in her lane. "How often do you fire this weapon?"

"At least once a year."

"That's not nearly enough to feel comfortable holding and aiming." He demonstrated the proper technique for holding a pistol and then had her show him the same.

"How's it been here at the Lonesome Pine since you turned it into a big game hunting ranch?" Grace asked.

"Business is good," he answered, his tone clipped.

Grace lined up her sites with the target. "Lot of people from out of state?" She squeezed the trigger, remembering not to anticipate the sound and slight movement of the gun. The pungent scent of gunpowder reminded her of her father and the first time he'd taken her out to shoot. As his only daughter, he wanted her to be safe and know how to defend herself should she have to. Her heart squeezed hard in her chest. Her father would be horrified to know she'd been the target of a killer. He'd be on the first plane back to Wyoming from their retirement home in Florida.

Grace refused to call them and tell them she was in trouble. They'd fly back in an instant and place themselves in the line of fire. She'd be damned if she let some low-life killer touch her family. Now if only she could stay alive so they didn't come back to a funeral.

She studied Wayne Batson out of the corner of her eye.

He was tall, muscular and lean. The man would have been incredibly handsome, but for the slight sneer on his lip that pushed him past handsome to annoyingly arrogant.

She fired several rounds, adjusting her aim, working for a tighter grouping.

Batson holstered his gun and turned toward Caveman. "Do you have any questions?"

Caveman gave him a friendly smile. "I have one. Do you have many locals come out to fire on your range, or is it mainly the out-of-towners?"

Grace ejected her magazine and made slow work of loading bullets, wanting to hear every word of the conversation between Batson and Caveman.

"I get locals who need a place to practice with real targets at specific distances. They come to improve their skills for hunting season, just like my out-of-towners. The only difference is that the locals can come more often."

"How do you keep the game contained inside the perimeter?" Caveman asked, while reloading his magazine.

"You might have noticed on your drive in, we have high fences surrounding all ten thousand acres. It's one of the largest fully contained game ranches in the state. We offer guided hunts of all kinds."

"A client could select the preferred prey?"

Batson nodded. "My clients can be very specific."

"You've stocked the ranch with animals, and they can choose what they want to hunt?" Caveman asked.

"Yes."

Caveman smacked the magazine into the grip of his pistol and stared across at Batson. "The fences keep all of them in?"

"Only the best materials were used," Batson said. "We have high-tech monitoring to detect breeches so that we can get to the exact location and fix them quickly."

"That had to cost," Grace said.

"My clients pay."

"Then why bother with a range like this if your big game hunts are paying the bills?"

"I've learned diversification is important. When all we had were cattle and horses, we had some hard times. I almost lost the ranch to the government for back taxes. I promised myself I'd never get in that situation again. I will not let the government take my family home, like they're trying to take the Vanderses'."

"You sound pretty adamant," Grace said.

Batson's jaw tightened. "I am."

Grace fit her magazine in the grip of her handgun and slammed it home. She stared down the barrel at the target and squeezed the trigger. Five rounds fired made five little holes on the silhouette target where the heart would be on a man. All her father's lessons came back with a little practice.

"Nice," Caveman commented. He brought his weapon up, aiming it downrange. "One other question for you, Mr. Batson."

"Shoot."

Caveman fired five rounds, hitting the silhouette target in the head, the holes the bullets made in such a tight grouping they appeared to be one big hole. He turned toward Batson with a friendly smile. "What do you prefer, handgun or rifle?"

Grace had been ejecting her magazine from her pistol. When she heard Caveman's unexpected question, she fumbled the magazine and it fell to the dirt.

Batson's eyes narrowed. For a moment, Grace didn't think the game ranch owner would answer the question.

"It depends on several things—how close I plan to get to the target, how accurate I want to be and how intelligent my quarry is." He touched a hand to his ear where he had a very small Bluetooth earpiece. "What is it, Laura?" He listened for a moment and then spoke. "Fine, let them in." His gaze returned to Grace. "Pardon me. It seems the sheriff wants to see me."

"The timing couldn't be better," Caveman said. "It's starting to get dark and we need to head back to town."

"Good." Batson nodded. "I don't usually leave guests on the range without supervision."

"Then we'll head out." Grace left the magazine out of her pistol, pulled back the bolt and inspected the chamber to make sure it was empty. Then she laid the weapon in its case.

"Thank you for allowing us to come out on such short notice."

They shook hands with Batson and stowed the gun cases in the backseat of Caveman's truck.

The sheriff's vehicle was pulling up as they drove away. Grace slowed and started to lower her window.

"Just wave and keep driving," Caveman advised.

"Won't the sheriff think that strange?"

"I'm not concerned about what the sheriff thinks." Caveman waved her forward. "I want to use the time he keeps Batson occupied to leave slowly and capture as much information as I can about the security system used around the perimeter."

Grace slowed, nodded and pulled past the sheriff as she headed down the road toward the gate.

Caveman studied the fences and the gate, making comments aloud about the cameras located at the top of the gate pillar, aimed at the road.

Once they were through the gate, Grace crept along the highway, moving slowly enough

Caveman could study the fencing. "I didn't notice it before, but stop for a minute."

Grace glanced in the rearview mirror. Nobody was behind her so she pulled to the side of the road and stopped. "Why are we stopping?"

"I want to test a theory." He opened his door, reached toward the ground and came up with a rock the size of a golf ball. Then he tossed it toward the fence wire. When the rock hit the fence, a shower of sparks shot out.

Grace gasped. "It's electric."

"Pretty expensive fencing for a game ranch."

"That'll keep the game in," Grace said.

Caveman's eyes narrowed to slits. "And uninvited guests out."

Wayne Batson had more than a game ranch on his huge spread: he had a locked-down compound capable of keeping out nosy people. As Grace drove back to town, a chill spread over her body. Her friendly community of Grizzly Pass had a darker side she never knew existed.

Chapter Thirteen

It was late by the time Caveman finished debriefing the team. He learned Kevin had sent the sheriff out to the Lonesome Pine Ranch to run interference for them so that they could leave unimpeded.

"While you two were on the inside, we had a drone flying over," Kevin said. "Between the information you two collected and the footage from the drone, we'll have our hands full tonight, determining the best way we can get in before the meeting tomorrow."

"Could we grab a bite to eat before we start?" Caveman asked.

"We can do better than that," Kevin said. He held out a key. "I got you two a suite at Mama Jo's Bed-and-Breakfast a couple blocks away.

You can eat, catch some sleep and come back in the morning to see what we found."

"You don't need us?" Grace asked.

"With four of us looking at the monitors, it will be crowded enough. And you two have already done enough. Get some food and rest. Tomorrow will be another day. We'll brief you on the plan then."

Hack chuckled. "We hope to *have* one by then. I anticipate pulling an all-nighter."

Caveman would have liked to have stayed and looked over the drone images, but he was hungry, and he bet Grace was, too.

They called down to the tavern and ordered carryout. A few minutes later they left the team, collected their food and drove to the quaint Victorian house just off Main Street. They had all of the second floor, which consisted of two bedrooms, a shared bathroom and a sitting room, complete with a television and a small dining table.

"I'm going to hit the shower before I eat," Grace said. "I feel dusty from being out on the range this afternoon."

"Want company?" Caveman asked.

"What do you think?" She smiled, dragged her shirt up over her head and dropped it on

the floor. Turning, she walked into the bathroom, half closed the door and then dangled
her bra through the opening.

Caveman was already halfway out of his
clothes, tripping over his boots as he kicked
them off.

The next minute, he was in the shower with
Grace, lathering her body, rinsing, kissing and
repeating the process until they had the bathroom steaming. They made love under the
warm spray and stayed until the water chilled.
By the time they'd dried, the night had settled
in on Grizzly Pass. Traffic slowed on Main
Street and folks went home to their families.

Caveman and Grace ate their dinner and
then moved to the king-size bed where they
made love again. Nearing midnight, they lay
in each other's arms, sated, but not sleepy.

"We should go back to the operations center
and see if they've discovered anything new,"
Grace said.

Caveman sighed and brushed his lips across
hers. "I know you're right. But I can't help it. I
don't want our time together to end."

"Me, either." She sighed, too, and kissed
him hard.

He would have stayed right where he was,

with Grace's warm body pressed against his, but they weren't done for the night. Caveman rolled out of the bed and extended his hand. "Ready?"

She shook her head, laid her hand in his and let him pull her to her feet. "I'll only be a minute." Grace grabbed her clothes and hurried into the bathroom.

"I'll call and let Kevin know we're coming," Caveman said. He made the call to learn Kevin, Hack, Ghost, T-Rex and Hawkeye were still up and poring over the videos. They'd noted a few items of interest they wanted to show Caveman. "Good," he said. "We'll be there soon."

He dressed quickly, pulled on his boots and waited by the window. From their room, he had a good view of Main Street and the front of Quincy Kemp's meat packing shop. It was dark, like most of the businesses in town at that hour. He wondered what was in the back of Quincy's shop that the man hadn't wanted Caveman to see. Could he have the wolf carcass, preparing it to be stuffed? And, if he did, he would know who killed it. Or was he hiding the AR-15s in one of his freezers behind big slabs of meat?

Dressed in a black turtleneck shirt and black jeans, Grace stepped up beside him and looked through the window. "What are you looking at?"

"Quincy's place. I went there while you were with Mrs. Penders. He didn't want me in the back of his building. He was pretty adamant about it. Which makes me think he has something to hide."

"What are you thinking?" She pulled on her boots and straightened. "Want to go there first?"

"I can send another member of the team to investigate."

"Why? They have enough on their plates. Obviously, Kemp isn't in his shop now. Not with all of the lights out, and no one moving around. We could get in, do a little spying and leave with no one the wiser."

His lips quirked on the corners. "You realize you're talking about breaking and entering."

"We're not stealing anything," Grace argued.

"It's still illegal."

"You're right." She chewed on her bottom lip. "You can't afford to be caught. It might get you in trouble with the military."

He didn't like the calculating look in her eyes. "What are you thinking?"

"That I'm brilliant, and you don't have to commit a crime. You could keep watch outside while I go in and poke around. That way you aren't in on the crime. If I'm caught, I'll be the only one charged."

"Have you heard of aiding and abetting?" Caveman countered.

She shrugged. "You just have to deny everything. I'll tell them I snuck off, leaving you wondering where I'd gone. It will all be on me."

"I'm surprised you would even consider it." He reached for her hand. "I took you for a by-the-books kind of woman."

Her lips thinned into a tight line. "I was, until someone started shooting at me. Desperate times call for...you know."

"Desperate measures." Caveman didn't like Grace's plan at all, but his gut told him Quincy was hiding something in the back of his shop. "Look, you're not going anywhere without me."

She smiled up at him, her brows rising in challenge. "Then I guess you'll be breaking the law with me, because I'm going into Quincy's place to see what he was hiding from you."

He slipped his arm around her waist and kissed her. "You're a stubborn woman, Grace Saunders."

"I have to be in my line of business."

"I'll bet you do." He kissed her again and then turned to scan what he could see of the street and buildings around Quincy's shop. Other than the tavern, the town of Grizzly Pass had more or less rolled up its sidewalks.

Grace headed for the door. "If we're going to do this, we should get moving."

Caveman shrugged into his jacket and followed. "Stay close."

"I told you, I don't like you playing the role of my bullet shield." She pulled on a dark coat and swept her hair up into a ponytail.

"Humor me, will you?" He grabbed her hand and led her out of the bed-and-breakfast, hugging the shadows of the building to the corner where it connected to Main Street. The road was clear of people and vehicles as far as Caveman could tell, but he didn't know who might be watching from any of the buildings.

"Come on." He looped his arm over her

shoulder and pulled her close. "We're just lovers on a late-night stroll."

"I like the sound of that," Grace whispered. "It would be even better if we weren't on someone's hot target list."

They crossed the street and walked past Quincy's place, turned down the next street and slipped into the back alley behind the meat packaging store.

Fortunately, the light over the back entrance was burned out, leaving the area completely in shadows.

Caveman slipped a knife from his pocket and pushed the blade in between the door and the jamb. With a few jiggles, he disengaged the lock, opened the door and hurried both of them inside.

Grace lifted her cell phone and shone the built-in flashlight around the room. The very back of the building was the meat packaging area with stainless-steel tables, sinks and refrigerators. The scents of blood, raw meat and disinfectants warred with each other.

Caveman checked the big walk-in freezers first. Finding nothing inside other than slabs of meat and big carcasses, he closed the doors. A quick survey of the rest of the room revealed nothing unusual or suspicious.

Quickly moving on, he led the way to a long corridor with a door on either side. This area separated the meat processing operations from the taxidermy workroom. He tried the handles. One was locked, the other wasn't. He pushed it open, only to find a variety of cleaning supplies: mops, aprons, bottles of disinfectant and various packaging supplies. The room was nothing more than a closet with shelves. Caveman checked the walls and floors for hidden doors.

"Anything?" Grace asked from the hall.

"Nothing." He left the supplies closet, locking it behind him.

Moving to the door across the way, Caveman used his knife to disengage the lock. Inside, he found an office with a desk, file cabinet and shelves. This room wasn't much bigger than the janitor's closet. Neither room was as wide as the shop front or the meat processing rear.

Caveman exited the office for a moment and walked into the taxidermy work area. It was as wide as the meat processing area, but square.

Grace gasped.

"What's wrong?"

She pointed to the hide of what appeared to be a black wolf. Tears welled in her eyes. "Loki." She shook her head, her fists bunching. "The bastard killed Loki."

Caveman pulled her against him and held her for a brief moment. "I'm sorry. But we have to keep moving."

"I know." She wiped a tear from her cheek and pushed away, turning her back to the wolf she'd raised from a pup.

Caveman's heart pinched at her sadness, but they had bigger, more immediate problems. "The office and supply room aren't as deep as the two work rooms. Where's the rest of the space?"

He hurried back into the office and checked the walls. In the back corner, on the far side of a large filing cabinet, was a wall with a pegboard attached. On the board, different tools hung neatly. Everywhere else in the office boxes were stacked on the floor, blocking access to the walls, except in front of the pegboard lined with tools.

Caveman pushed the pegboard and the entire wall moved just a little. He tapped on the wall, creating a hollow sound. Running his fingers along the outer edge of the pegboard he traced one end and then the other. Halfway down the right side, his finger encountered a hidden latch. He released it and the pegboard and wall swung toward him.

"I'll be damned," Grace muttered behind him.

He glanced back at the woman standing in the doorway of the office. "Could you keep an eye on the hallway while I go in to check it out?"

Grace nodded. "Okay, but don't be too long." She shot a nervous glance over her shoulder. "I have a bad feeling about this."

"I'll hurry." He ducked into the room, shining his cell phone flashlight at the far walls, looking for windows to the outside. When he didn't locate any, he flipped the light switch on the wall and studied the contents of the room, his stomach clenching into a vicious knot.

Racks filled with guns stood in short, neat rows. Shelves lined the walls loaded with boxes of ammunition.

"I think I found at least half of the AR-15s here in this room."

"Uh, Max…" Grace's voice sounded strained behind him, closer than if she'd been in the hallway. "We have a problem."

Caveman turned to face her.

She stood with her head tilted backward, a darkly clothed arm wrapped around her neck, her eyes wide and frightened.

In the split second it took Caveman to realize what had happened, he was already too late.

Two probes hit him in the chest and a charge of electricity ripped through his body. He clenched his teeth to keep from crying out. Then he fell, his muscles refusing to hold up his frame.

"Caveman!" Grace screamed.

Unable to control his fall, he hit his head against the corner of a low cabinet and blackness engulfed him in a shroud of darkness and pain.

GRACE FOUGHT AGAINST the hands holding her, desperate to get to Caveman.

The man with the Taser moved forward, his head and face concealed in a ski mask, his hands in leather gloves. He yanked Caveman's wrists together behind his back and slipped a zip tie around them, cinching it tightly. Then he rolled Caveman onto his side, pulled the probes out of his chest and nodded. "He's down."

A jagged cut on Caveman's temple oozed blood onto the floor.

Grace wanted to go to him, but the man holding her was so much stronger than she was, and his arm around her throat squeezed just hard enough to limit her air intake. Gray fog crept in on the corners of her vision. *No.* She couldn't pass out. She had to find a way to extricate herself and Caveman from this dangerous situation.

"What do we do with them?" one of the men asked.

"Boss wants them." Even with the mask, the man was easy to recognize just by his low, gravelly voice.

"Quincy," Grace said. "Don't do this. You won't get away with it."

"Shut up." Quincy backhanded her, his knuckles slamming into her cheekbone.

Grace's head whipped back with the blow and pain knifed through her. She fought the dizzying spinning in her head that threatened to take her down. "What are you going to do with us?"

"That's not for me to decide," he said.

"So you do the dirty work of capturing us,

committing a crime to do it, and your boss sits back and lets you take the rap?"

He backhanded her again, this time hitting her in the mouth, splitting her lip. "You should have stayed out of this. Now, you'll pay the price for meddling."

Her jaw ached and the coppery taste of blood invaded her mouth. Anger roiled inside, pushing aside the wobbly feeling of an oncoming faint.

Caveman lay on the floor, his body still, and Grace could do nothing. The man holding her was a lot bigger and stronger. And there were two of them to one of her. Outnumbered and overpowered, she didn't have a choice. But she had to do something.

"You know you won't get away with this. There's probably a sheriff's deputy driving by as we speak."

Quincy's lip curled back in a snarl. "No one knows you're back here, and no one can see inside this part of the building. Even if the police came in, I'd be legally in the right. You two trespassed on private property. Last I checked, breaking and entering was illegal. I could shoot you and claim self-defense. Now, enough talk." He shoved a rag in her mouth, then threw a pillowcase over her head and down her arms. "Take her out to the van."

The big man holding her scooped her off her feet, slung her over his shoulder where she landed hard on her belly, the breath knocked out of her lungs. She couldn't see anything through the fabric of the pillowcase, but she could tell the man was carrying her back the way they'd entered the shop. When they stepped out of the building, cool night air wrapped around her legs. The sound of a metal door sliding sideways gave her renewed determination to break free. She kicked and struggled, bucking in the man's grip.

Finally, she was flung away from him, landing on what she was sure was the floorboard of a commercial van. She hit the surface hard, her head bouncing off the metal.

Then something was stuck up against her arm and a jolt of electricity sliced through her. Her body went limp and her struggles ceased. But she could still tell a little of what was going on. Someone tied her wrists behind her back with a zip tie. Another body was dumped onto the floor beside her.

It had to be Caveman.

With her wrists bound and a pillowcase

wrapped loosely around her head, her body in a catatonic state, she could do little to free herself or her head so that she could see. She vowed that as soon as she regained control of her muscles, she'd work her way out of the case and zip tie.

Meanwhile, she was conscious. She listened, trying to gauge which direction they were headed and how far they were going. She could tell when they left the back alley and emerged on paved highway. She guessed they were headed south on Main Street. If only she could get up, throw open the door and scream. Alas, she could barely wiggle her toes by the time she was certain they'd driven out of the little town.

Would they take them out to a remote location, shoot them and leave their bodies to rot?

Grace's chest tightened. She couldn't let that happen. All of this was her fault. If she hadn't witnessed the killer shooting at Mr. Khalig, none of this would be happening to her and Caveman.

Caveman.

He was the innocent bystander in all of this. And because she'd allowed him to get past the walls she'd erected around her heart, he would die.

She squeezed her fist, anger fueling her. When her toes tingled, she wiggled them. Slowly, the feeling came back to her legs and arms. She was able to roll onto her side, but she couldn't lift her arms to pull off the pillowcase. Instead, she scooted along the floor, trying to maneuver her way out of the fabric covering her head.

They had been traveling ten minutes when she finally made it out of the pillowcase.

Lifting her head, she looked around the interior of an empty utility van with metal sides and floors. The two men who'd captured them sat in the front seat, staring out the window as they slowed for a stop.

Grace tried to see what they were seeing. It appeared to be a gate of some sort.

The van lurched forward and the tires crunched on what sounded like gravel.

With little light to see by, Grace searched the interior of the van for something sharp to break the zip tie holding her wrists tightly together behind her. No sharp edges stuck out, no tools lay on the metal floor.

And Caveman lay as still as death.

She inched her way over to him and laid her face close to his. For a long moment she held her breath, praying he was still alive. Then she felt the warmth of his breath against her cheek. Her heart swelled with joy. He was still alive.

Somehow, she had to get them both out of the van and away from their captors.

The gravel road ended, but the van continued to move forward on a much bumpier, hard-packed road.

Several times, Grace tried to sit up, only to be flung across the van floor. She was better off lying on her side, praying they'd stop before she was bounced to death.

Caveman groaned softly and his legs moved. "Grace?" he whispered.

"I'm here," she replied softly, so as not to draw attention from the men in the front seats.

"Where are we?"

"We're in the back of a van and have been on the road for over twenty minutes as far as I can guess. Other than that, I'm not sure where we are. Based on the road conditions, I'd bet we're way out in the boondocks."

"Have they said what they're going to do with us?"

"No." She glanced at the back of the driver's

head. "Quincy said something about it wasn't up to them. The boss would decide."

"So he's not in charge."

The van came to a jerky stop.

Grace waited for them to start up again, but they didn't. The engine switched off and the two men climbed out. A moment later, the side door slid open and moonlight shone into the interior.

Grace blinked up at the men.

Quincy had taken off his ski mask, but the other man hadn't. They grabbed Grace by her upper arms and dragged her out of the van and onto her feet.

"Hurt her, and I'll kill you," Caveman said, his voice little more than a feral growl.

Quincy snorted. "That would be really hard to do when you're all tied up, now wouldn't it?"

They grabbed Caveman by the arms and slid him out of the van, dumping him on the ground at their feet.

He rolled to his side, bunched his legs and pushed to his feet. "What now?"

"Now, the fun begins," another voice said from behind Quincy and his accomplice. A big man wearing a combat helmet, camouflage clothing and carrying a military-grade rifle stepped between their two captors. His face was blackened with paint and he sported a pair of what appeared to be night-vision goggles pushed up onto his helmet.

"What do you mean, 'now the fun begins'?"

"I told you. I provide all kinds of prey for my clients—elk, lion, moose, bear and…human."

Grace gasped, a heavy, sick feeling filling her belly. "You can't be serious."

"Oh, I'm serious, all right."

Grace squinted, trying to see past the paint. "Wayne?"

The man sneered. "Surprised?"

"Actually, I am." She shook her head. "Why would you risk losing everything you have by killing people? You won't get away with it for long?"

"I've been getting away with it for the past five years. I'll continue to get away with it as long as no one finds the bodies. *Your* bodies."

"You're insane."

"No, I'm tired of the government stealing what's mine. I'm tired of working my butt off for the pittance you make off cattle, only for the government to steal every cent I make by charging an insane amount of taxes."

"You've been selling human hunts for the

past five years?" Grace shook her head. "How did no one know this?"

"The people who work for me know not to say anything. And the people we hunt don't live long enough to tell."

"Was Mr. Khalig one of your *hunts*?" Grace's stomach churned so hard she fought to keep from losing her dinner.

Wayne snorted. "Hell no. He was a paid gig. And an easy target."

"Paid gig?" What was wrong with the man? He acted like killing a man was no worse than being paid to perform on stage.

"*Highly* paid gig." Wayne shifted his rifle to his other hand. "But that's not why we're here tonight."

"Why are we here?" Caveman asked, his gaze direct, the shadows cast by the bright moon making him appear dangerous.

"You two are going to be a little training opportunity for my men. A little night ops search-and-destroy. You get a chance to run. They get to practice and test their night hunting skills with live animals."

"That's like shooting lions in a zoo. Where's the sport in that?"

"Oh, there will be sport. We're going to let

you loose, give you a little bit of a head start, and then we're coming after you."

"Unarmed?" Caveman goaded. "How is that a training exercise?"

"I can't turn over a loaded weapon to a trained soldier. How would we explain so many people with gunshot wounds?" Wayne nodded to Quincy. "Release them."

Quincy frowned. "Now?"

"Now." Wayne fixed his stare on Caveman. "If you make a move toward me or my men, I'll put a bullet in Ms. Saunders." He nodded. "Take her and leave. You'll only have five minutes to get as far as you can, before we come after you." He glanced down at his watch.

"Three minutes on foot won't get us far," Caveman pointed out.

"You're lucky I'm giving you that." He looked again at his watch. "Four minutes thirty-five seconds."

"Aren't you going to cut the zip ties?" Grace's pulse hammered so loudly in her ears she could barely hear herself think.

"Not my problem." Wayne Batson raised his brows. "Four minutes fifteen seconds."

"Grace, come on." Caveman pushed her with his elbow and herded her away from Batson.

She hurried with Caveman toward the tree line. Her last glimpse of the three hunters was the image of Quincy and the other man dressed in the combat helmet, multi-pocketed vests and camouflage clothing. They were in the process of loading ammunition magazines into their vests.

And she thought getting away from the men would be hard enough. *Staying* away from Wayne Batson and his thugs, while their hands were tied behind their backs, would be a lot more of a challenge than she could imagine.

Chapter Fourteen

They jogged into the tree line. Caveman's leg hurt like hell, but he refused to slow them down. "We have to get as far away from them as possible and find a rock hill or cliff to put between us and them. Are you able to run for long?"

"I can hold my own," Grace said. "I'm used to hiking in the hills. When I'm not working, I train to run half marathons."

Caveman snorted. "I'll have a hard time keeping up with you. Why don't you lead the way?"

"Do you think we're on Batson's ranch?" she asked, jogging alongside Caveman while they were on a fairly wide path between trees.

"That's my bet. Not only do those fences keep people out, they keep his pets in."

"Any chance we can get out of these zip ties?" she asked.

"As soon as we reach that outcropping of rocks. We have to put something solid and impenetrable between us and them for cover as well as concealment against their night-vision goggles." He glanced across at her face in the moonlight. "Can you run faster?"

"I'm game," she said, though her breathing had become more labored.

Caveman increased his speed, glancing back often enough to make certain Grace kept up. He was aiming for the base of the mountain he'd glimpsed through gaps in the trees. It appeared to be right in front of them, but looks could be deceiving, especially at night.

The full moon helped them find their way, but it also made it all too easy for Batson and his gang to see them. The sooner they made it into the hills, the better.

He figured the five-minute head start had long since expired and still they hadn't reached the relative safety of the mountain.

A crash behind him brought Caveman to a halt.

Grace lay on the ground, struggling to get

to her feet. "Don't wait on me. I'll catch up," she insisted.

"Like hell you will." He squatted next to her. "Grab a sturdy tree branch or a jagged rock."

She did, rolled over to hand it to him and then worked herself to a sitting position. "What are you going to do with it?"

"I'm going to try and use it as a saw." He nodded. "But we have to keep moving. Lean on me to get up."

She leaned her shoulder against him and pushed herself to stand.

"Ready?" he said.

"Go." Grace followed him, keeping closer this time.

While he ran, Caveman rubbed the small tree branch against the plastic of the zip tie. It wasn't much, but he hoped with enough friction, it would eventually cut through.

They emerged in a small opening in the forest, finding themselves at the base of a bluff.

Caveman glanced each direction, then turned north toward a large outcropping of boulders. If they could get behind them, they could stop long enough to break the zip ties. But they couldn't stay long. They had to go deep into the mountains and stay alive long enough for

Kevin and the team to figure out they were in trouble.

A sinking feeling settled low in his belly. Though he'd given Kevin a heads-up that they'd be over to review drone footage, he hadn't given him a definitive time. All they could hope for was that Kevin would get worried when they didn't show up within thirty minutes of the call. Still, the team wouldn't know where they'd gone, or where to start looking.

Their best bet was to avoid the hunters long enough to make it back to one of the perimeter fences. Then they'd have to figure out how to get through it and fast enough they could make it to a road and catch a ride to town. Timing would be crucial since Batson had the fence wired to tell him exactly where the breech occurred.

Caveman kept his thoughts to himself. Grace had enough to worry about just staying a step ahead of Batson and his gang.

In order for them to reach the giant boulders for cover, they would have to cross a wide-open expanse, flooded by bright moonlight.

"I don't know how close they are. When we start out across the open area, run as fast as you can and zigzag to make it harder for someone to sight in on you." He gripped Grace's arms. "Are you okay?"

She nodded, breathing hard. "I'll be fine. Let's go." With a deep breath, she took off running across the rocky terrain, dodging back and forth, leaping over brush and smaller boulders.

Caveman was right behind her, hoping the hunters hadn't yet caught up to them.

A shot rang out, kicking up the dirt near Caveman's feet. He ran faster, changing directions erratically, hoping the gunmen couldn't get a bead on him and take him out.

Grace had just made it to the boulder when another shot rang out. She stumbled and fell against the huge rock, righted herself and slipped out of sight.

Caveman dodged once more to the right, then sprinted the remaining ten steps and dove behind the boulder.

Grace was on her knees, breathing hard, but rubbing the zip tie against a jagged stone jutting out of the hillside.

"We don't have time to break these. We have to keep moving," Caveman warned.

The zip tie snapped. "I'm ready." She grabbed

a sharp rock and pointed to a flat one. "Put your hands here." She quickly positioned him, then put all of her weight behind the sharp rock and cut through his zip tie.

Caveman took her hand and ran for a ravine thirty feet from where they were standing. Together, they climbed the side of the hill, working their way over the rocks upward to a ridge. If they could drop over the other side, they'd have a chance of staying out of range of the rifles. He wasn't sure how much longer Grace would last. His sore leg ached and he worried it slowed him down too much. They didn't have weapons and they couldn't fight back. He had to keep them moving.

Grace slipped beside him and slid several feet down the hillside and stopped abruptly when her foot hit a tree root. "Damn." She doubled over, clutching at her leg. She pushed to her feet, but fell back as soon as she put weight on her foot.

Caveman slid down next to her, his gaze scanning the bottom of the ravine. "What's wrong?"

"I think I've sprained my ankle." She looked up at him. "Don't stop. You have to keep going. Get help."

He pressed his lips together. "Grace, I'm not leaving without you." He bent, draped her arm over his shoulder and lifted her. "Come on. We're not stopping here."

Together, they limped up the side of the steep hill, slipping and sliding on the loose gravel. When they reached the top of the ridge, Caveman studied the other side. There was a steep drop-off close to where they stood and a trail leading down the other side. If they were careful, they might make it down to the bottom before the others caught up to them. From there, he could see the fence in the distance. And, if he wasn't mistaken, the cutaway between a stand of trees had to be the highway. "See that?"

"The fence," Grace said through gritted teeth. "Think we can make it?"

"I don't think it, I know it." With his arm around her waist, he hurried down the trail toward the bottom of the hill, knowing this trail was the path of least resistance and it would make it far too easy for the hunters to spot them from a distance and catch up to them all too quickly. They only had to get close enough to sight in on them.

A good sniper would be able to pick them

off at two-hundred meters. A great sniper would be able to take them out at four-hundred. If they could get down to the trees before the hunters topped the ridge, they might have a little more of a chance to make it to the fence. At that point, they'd have to figure out how to keep from getting electrocuted.

HOPPING ON ONE foot all the way down the side of a hill wasn't getting them where they needed to be fast enough. And every time she bumped her right foot, pain shot through her, bringing her close to tears. She refused to cry. Not when they needed every bit of their wits about them to escape the insanity that was Wayne Batson. "Leave me," she begged. "I don't want you to die because of me."

"Not up for discussion," he said, grunting as he took the brunt of her weight and hurried her along. "Save your breath and mine."

She knew any further argument would be ignored and took his advice to save him further aggravation. They rounded several hip-high boulders as they neared the bottom of the hill. A shot rang out and pinged off one of the boulders.

A sharp stinging sensation bit Grace's shoulder. "Ow!"

"Get down!" Caveman pulled her down behind the boulder. He looked ahead to the next big rock. "Can you crawl to the next one?"

"Probably faster than I could walk it by myself."

"Then go, while I distract them."

"What do you mean 'distract them'?" she asked, hesitant to leave him, even for a moment.

He shed his jacket and hung it on a stick. "Ready? Go!" He ran the stick up over the top of the rock.

Grace crawled as fast as she could over rocks, gravel and brush, bruising her knees, but not caring. When she made it to the next rock, she rolled behind it and called out, "Made it!" She sneaked a peek around the edge in time to see Caveman make his dash to join her.

He hunkered low and ran, diving behind the rock as two more shots echoed off the canyon walls. "Are you all right?" he asked, his attention on the hill above them.

"A little worse for the wear, but alive." She pressed a hand to the stinging spot on her shoulder and winced. When she brought her hand back in front of her, she grimaced. It was covered in dark warm liquid she suspected was her blood. She hid her hand from Caveman. If she was badly wounded, she wouldn't have been able to move her arm. Now wasn't the time to faint at the sight of blood.

"Right now, they have the advantage with their night-vision goggles. They can see us, but we can't see them."

She snorted. "They have all the advantages. They have the guns. We're unarmed."

He glanced behind them. "We could try for the tree line, but it's a long way."

"And I move too slowly." She shook her head. "Leave me here. Go for help. It's the only way."

"I'm not leaving you."

"Then what do you suggest?"

He glanced around the moonlit area. "The fence is two football fields away. Even if we could make it there, we don't have a way to cut through."

"Then that's out," she said.

"We've run out of places to hide. This is the last large boulder between us and them."

"True."

"We only have one choice." He drew in a

deep breath and let it out. "We wait until they come to us."

Grace nodded, knowing the odds were stacked against them, but unwilling to admit defeat. She wouldn't go down without a helluva fight. "Then we have to be prepared."

"You're willing to stick it out?"

She chuckled. Her ankle hurt like hell, she was bleeding and she didn't know if she'd live to see another sunrise. "Seems like our only recourse. So, Army Special Forces dude, what can we do to get ready to rumble?"

"Stay here."

She laughed out loud. "Like I could get up and dance a jig?"

"You know what I mean. Don't poke your head out. Stay behind the rock so that I don't have to worry about what's happening while I'm not here."

She frowned. "Not here? Where are you going?" Grace reached out and touched his arm. "You can't leave the safety of the boulder. They'll shoot you."

He took her hand in his and looked down into her eyes. "I'm not dying today. I'm going to debunk your curse."

"Sweetheart, I hope and pray you do." She

wrapped her other arm around his neck and pulled him close. "I'd really like to spend a little more time with you. Two days is not nearly enough."

"I'm thinking a life time won't be enough." He kissed her hard, his tongue sweeping across hers. Then he pulled away. "Now, I have to see what I can come up with. I'll be back."

"I'm counting on it," Grace whispered.

The night stood still. Not even the crickets or coyotes sang in the dark.

Caveman got up on his haunches, breathed in and out, then dove toward a stand of trees nearby.

The crack of gunfire rang out.

Grace flinched and strained her eyes, searching for movement in the shadows. She could hear the crunch of leaves and the snapping of sticks. Caveman was moving.

Another shot pierced the silence. This one seemed closer, though it was hard to tell when the sound bounced off the hillsides.

With her breath lodged in her throat, Grace waited for Caveman's return. She gathered stones, rocks and anything she could use as a weapon, no matter how puny they seemed compared to a high-powered rifle. She even scraped up a pile of sand next to her.

Then Caveman came running toward her. Just as he was about to make it behind the boulder, gunfire sounded so close, Grace yelped.

Caveman fell behind the boulder, his arms loaded with sticks and what looked like half a tree. He lay still for a moment, his breathing ragged.

"Are you okay?" Grace crawled toward him, pushing aside the sticks and brush.

"I'm fine, just winded." He drew himself up to a sitting position. "They're getting closer." He handed her several long sticks. "They aren't much, but you can use them like spears. The hunters have to come around the boulder to get to us. That's when we surprise them with these."

"What if they swing wide?"

"Hey, I'm trying to be positive. Help me out." He kissed her cheek. "Seriously, we could do with the power of positive thinking. It's just about all we have left."

"Okay, I'm positive they can swing wide and stay out of spear range, but I'm willing to try anything. I'm not ready to leave this world."

"Good, because we're going to play dead," Caveman said.

"What?"

"You heard me. We're going to play dead. It's risky, but we don't have any other way to lure them in." He grabbed some of the bigger rocks and stones, placing them in circle around them where the boulder would not provide protection. "We'll lie as flat as we can against the ground, thus we won't present much of a target. They will have to come closer to finish us off. That's when we hit them. Got it?"

"Got it."

"Now, before they get any closer, we need to assume the dead cockroach position with our spears at our side." He waited while she lay on her back, her hand on her the spear.

Grace's pulse thumped hard in her veins, her breath came in shaky gasps. In her mind, she told herself she was not ready to die. She wanted to live. To kiss Caveman and make love to him again in the comfort of a bed.

"Shh." Caveman pressed a finger to his lips and laid down beside her. "They're coming."

Grace lay as still as death, her breath caught in her throat, trying not to make even the sound of her breathing.

As she remained there counting what could possibly be the last beats of her heart, she heard another sound. A *thump, thump, thumping* sound that started out soft, but grew louder with each passing minute.

"What the hell?" Caveman started to sit up. The crack of a gunshot sounded so close, it could have been right beside them.

Caveman dropped back down on his back and groaned loudly.

"Are you okay?" Grace whispered.

"I'm fine. That was for effect."

The thumping grew louder. "What's that sound?"

"I hope it's what I think it is."

"What?"

"The cavalry arriving to save the day."

Another shot rang out, and another, each getting closer. One kicked up rocks near Grace's hand. Another pinged against the boulder, ricocheted off the surface and hit the ground so near to her head she swore she could feel the whoosh of air.

Grace finally recognized the thumping sound as that of helicopter rotors churning the air. A bright light pierced the night, shining down to the ground.

"Stay down," Caveman said. "That light will make their night-vision goggles useless. I'm going after them."

"But you're unarmed," she cried out. She rolled onto her stomach and watched as Caveman disappeared into the darkness surround the ray of light.

A burst of gunfire ripped through the air, followed by an answering burst from the helicopter above.

Grace rose to her knees, her heart in her throat. Where was Caveman?

Chapter Fifteen

The helicopter was taking on fire. Caveman didn't want to get in the way as they fired back. He watched as the beam of light played over the ground.

There. One of the men stood near a tree, aiming his weapon toward the chopper.

Caveman was torn between going after him and staying close to Grace. If he let the man shoot at the helicopter, he could kill the men inside and possibly bring the helicopter down. A burst of semiautomatic gunfire erupted from the aircraft. The man caught in the beam of light dropped to the ground and lay still.

More shots rang out.

Caveman wanted to go after the hunters, but the light from the helicopter was blinding him, as well. Then a shot hit the bulb on the light and it blinked out. The chopper swung around and lowered to the ground.

Giving his eyes a few moments to adjust to the moonlight, Caveman hunkered low to the ground near a tree a couple yards from where Grace lay. A movement alerted him to someone moving nearby. He recognized the man as Quincy Kemp.

When the meat packer walked within three feet of Caveman's position, he raised his rifle, aiming at Grace.

Caveman swung the limb he'd been holding as hard as he could. The limb caught the man's arm, tipping the rifle upward as it went off.

Caveman struck again, catching Quincy in the chin, knocking him backward so forcefully he fell, hitting his head against a rock. The man didn't move.

Grabbing the rifle from the ground, Caveman searched the darkness for the last man standing. His gut told him it was Wayne Batson.

Shouts sounded off in the field near the helicopter. The silhouettes of men disengaged from that of the aircraft, all running toward Caveman's position. Still, he couldn't see

Wayne. Where had he gone? Had he run as soon as the helicopter showed up?

Then a movement near the giant boulder caught his attention. Wayne Batson stepped out of the shadows and pointed his rifle at Grace where she lay on the ground. "Come any closer and I kill the girl!"

Caveman froze, his heart slammed to a stop. *No. Not Grace!* He wanted to shout. But he was afraid any movement would push Batson over the edge and he'd pull the trigger. The man was crazy. You couldn't reason with crazy.

Batson reached down, bending over Grace's inert form. Then the ground beneath him erupted.

Grace jerked the spear she'd been holding up into the man's belly. She rolled to the side at the same time, sweeping her good leg out to catch Batson's.

Batson pitched forward, falling onto the makeshift spear. He screamed out loud, and pulled the trigger on his rifle. The shots hit the dirt. He toppled to the ground beside Grace, losing his hold on the weapon. Grace tried to get away, but the man grabbed a handful of her hair.

Caveman lunged forward, kicked the rifle

out of Batson's reach and slammed his foot into the man's face.

Batson flew backward, letting go of Grace's hair, and lay motionless.

Caveman scooped Grace up off the ground and held her in his arms, crushing her against him. "Sweet Jesus, woman. I thought I'd lost you!"

She wrapped her arms around his neck and pulled him close for a kiss. "I wasn't going anywhere without you. I told myself, I had to get out of this so that I could kiss you."

"Please. Kiss me all you want, because that's what I want, too."

"Caveman? Grace?" Kevin Garner's voice called out. "Are you two okay?"

Caveman broke off the kiss long enough to say, "We're alive." And he went back to kissing her.

"Are there anymore bogies? We counted three."

Grace broke their kiss this time. "Three were all there was. By the way. Thanks. Your timing was impeccable." She grinned at Kevin as the DHS man stepped out of the tree line and approached them.

"The sheriff's on his way," Hack said, emerging from the tree line, dressed in a bulletproof vest and helmet. He was carrying a satellite phone and an AR-15. "Thank goodness we decided to run the drone tonight, or we might not have found you."

Grace laughed. "Thank God for drones and Hack." She turned to Caveman. "As much as I love when you hold me close, you can set me on my own feet. Or foot."

Caveman shook his head. "If it's all the same to you, I'd rather get you back to town and have a doctor look at your ankle and that shoulder. You're bleeding all over me."

"Take the chopper," Kevin said. "We'll stay here and wait for the sheriff."

Caveman glanced across at Kevin. "Thanks."

Kevin smiled. "If you still want to go back to your unit at the end of the week, I'll make it happen."

Grace shot a look up at him.

Caveman shook his head. "If it's all the same to you, I'd like to stay and see this operation through to the end." His gaze dropped to Grace. "I'm just getting to know the locals. I'd like to get to know them a little better. Maybe something will come of it."

Kevin clapped a hand on his shoulder.

"Yeah. They have a way of growing on you. As you can see, we can use all the help we can get."

"Count me in," he said. "In the meantime, I'll see that Miss Saunders gets to a doctor."

"You do that. When you're both rested up, stop by the loft for a debriefing."

"You got it." Caveman carried Grace to the helicopter.

"Isn't your leg bothering you?" Grace asked.

"What leg? I don't feel a thing except the beat of my heart."

She snorted. "The Delta Force soldier is a closet poet?"

"Hey, don't knock it." He set her in the seat and buckled the seat belt around her, his fingers grazing her breasts. Then he handed her a headset, helping her to fit them over her ears.

He climbed in next to her, buckled his belt and positioned a headset over his ears.

"Where did Kevin get a helicopter?" Grace asked into her mic.

"I think it's the one they used in the hostage rescue." He leaned over the back of the seat toward the pilot. "How did you get here so quickly?"

"I was still in town, waiting for some replacement parts I got in today," the pilot said into the headset. "I was due to fly out tomorrow, but I think I'll be delayed yet again."

As the chopper rose from the ground, the gray light of predawn crept up to the edge of the peaks.

Caveman stared down at the men on the ground, standing guard over the hunters who'd gambled their lives on an evil sport and lost.

"Think they'll live to testify?" Grace asked, her voice crackling over the radio headset.

"I hope so. I'd like to know who paid Batson to shoot Khalig."

"Me, too."

"Somehow, I don't think we'll get that answer from Batson."

"No, he wasn't looking so good," Grace said, her face pale, her brow furrowed. "If he dies, that will be the first man I've ever killed."

"And hopefully the last."

Her lips firmed. "I refuse to feel bad about it. The man was pure evil."

"Agreed." He squeezed her hand. "In the meantime, I have more work to do. We still don't know why Mr. Khalig had been killed and who had paid Wayne Batson to do the job."

Grace nodded. "True."

Caveman tipped her chin up and stared down into her eyes. "Do you still believe you're cursed?"

Grace shrugged. "I have to admit, you dodged death enough in the past couple of hours it makes me think you're the only man who could possibly break the curse."

"You're not cursed."

"Okay. Maybe I'm not." She laid her hand in his, silence stretching between them. "Caveman?"

"Yes, sweetheart?" Despite talking into a radio, he'd never felt closer to her.

"Do you believe in love at first sight?" she asked.

"I didn't." He squeezed her hand and raised it to his lips. "Not until I met you."

"Excuse me," another voice sounded in Caveman's ear.

He shot a glance toward the pilot and grimaced.

"I hate to break up your little lovefest, Caveman, but we're about to land. I suggest you save the rest of it until you get her alone."

"Thanks, I will."

The chopper landed, Caveman climbed out

and lifted Grace out, but refused to set her on her feet until they were clear of the rotors.

Grace insisted they watch until the helicopter lifted off. Then she turned to Caveman. "Let's get to the doctor and back to the room. I think there's a shower calling my name."

"I hear my name in there, too."

"Darn right, you do."

He lifted her into his arms and kissed her, glad he'd been stuck with this strange assignment out in the wilds of Wyoming. This woman seemed to be his perfect match with the potential to be the love of his life. He planned on exploring that theory. One kiss at a time.

* * * * *

LARGER-PRINT BOOKS!

HARLEQUIN

Presents®

GET 2 FREE LARGER-PRINT NOVELS PLUS 2 FREE GIFTS!

PASSION
GUARANTEED
SEDUCTION

YES! Please send me 2 FREE LARGER-PRINT Harlequin Presents® novels and my 2 FREE gifts (gifts are worth about $10). After receiving them, if I don't wish to receive any more books, I can return the shipping statement marked "cancel." If I don't cancel, I will receive 6 brand-new novels every month and be billed just $5.30 per book in the U.S. or $5.74 per book in Canada. That's a saving of at least 12% off the cover price! It's quite a bargain! Shipping and handling is just 50¢ per book in the U.S. and 75¢ per book in Canada.* I understand that accepting the 2 free books and gifts places me under no obligation to buy anything. I can always return a shipment and cancel at any time. Even if I never buy another book, the two free books and gifts are mine to keep forever.

176/376 HDN GHVY

Name _____ (PLEASE PRINT)

Address _____ Apt. #

City _____ State/Prov. _____ Zip/Postal Code

Signature (if under 18, a parent or guardian must sign)

Mail to the **Reader Service:**
IN U.S.A.: P.O. Box 1867, Buffalo, NY 14240-1867
IN CANADA: P.O. Box 609, Fort Erie, Ontario L2A 5X3

**Are you a subscriber to Harlequin Presents® books
and want to receive the larger-print edition?
Call 1-800-873-8635 today or visit us at www.ReaderService.com.**

---

* Terms and prices subject to change without notice. Prices do not include applicable taxes. Sales tax applicable in N.Y. Canadian residents will be charged applicable taxes. Offer not valid in Quebec. This offer is limited to one order per household. Not valid for current subscribers to Harlequin Presents Larger-Print books. All orders subject to credit approval. Credit or debit balances in a customer's account(s) may be offset by any other outstanding balance owed by or to the customer. Please allow 4 to 6 weeks for delivery. Offer available while quantities last.

Your Privacy—The Reader Service is committed to protecting your privacy. Our Privacy Policy is available online at www.ReaderService.com or upon request from the Reader Service.

We make a portion of our mailing list available to reputable third parties that offer products we believe may interest you. If you prefer that we not exchange your name with third parties, or if you wish to clarify or modify your communication preferences, please visit us at www.ReaderService.com/consumerschoice or write to us at Reader Service Preference Service, P.O. Box 9062, Buffalo, NY 14240-9062. Include your complete name and address.

HPLP15

LARGER-PRINT BOOKS!
GET 2 FREE LARGER-PRINT NOVELS PLUS
2 FREE GIFTS!

◊ HARLEQUIN®

Romance

From the Heart, For the Heart

YES! Please send me 2 FREE LARGER-PRINT Harlequin® Romance novels and my 2 FREE gifts (gifts are worth about $10). After receiving them, if I don't wish to receive any more books, I can return the shipping statement marked "cancel." If I don't cancel, I will receive 4 brand-new novels every month and be billed just $5.09 per book in the U.S. or $5.49 per book in Canada. That's a savings of at least 15% off the cover price! It's quite a bargain! Shipping and handling is just 50¢ per book in the U.S. and 75¢ per book in Canada.* I understand that accepting the 2 free books and gifts places me under no obligation to buy anything. I can always return a shipment and cancel at any time. Even if I never buy another book, the two free books and gifts are mine to keep forever.

119/319 HDN GHWC

Name _____ (PLEASE PRINT)

Address _____ Apt. #

City _____ State/Prov. _____ Zip/Postal Code

Signature (if under 18, a parent or guardian must sign)

Mail to the **Reader Service:**
IN U.S.A.: P.O. Box 1867, Buffalo, NY 14240-1867
IN CANADA: P.O. Box 609, Fort Erie, Ontario L2A 5X3
Want to try two free books from another line?
Call 1-800-873-8635 or visit www.ReaderService.com.

* Terms and prices subject to change without notice. Prices do not include applicable taxes. Sales tax applicable in N.Y. Canadian residents will be charged applicable taxes. Offer not valid in Quebec. This offer is limited to one order per household. Not valid for current subscribers to Harlequin Romance Larger-Print books. All orders subject to credit approval. Credit or debit balances in a customer's account(s) may be offset by any other outstanding balance owed by or to the customer. Please allow 4 to 6 weeks for delivery. Offer available while quantities last.

Your Privacy—The Reader Service is committed to protecting your privacy. Our Privacy Policy is available online at www.ReaderService.com or upon request from the Reader Service.

We make a portion of our mailing list available to reputable third parties that offer products we believe may interest you. If you prefer that we not exchange your name with third parties, or if you wish to clarify or modify your communication preferences, please visit us at www.ReaderService.com/consumerschoice or write to us at Reader Service Preference Service, P.O. Box 9062, Buffalo, NY 14240-9062. Include your complete name and address.

HRLP15

WESTERN WP PROMISES

YES! Please send me **The Western Promises Collection** in Larger Print. This collection begins with 3 FREE books and 2 FREE gifts (gifts valued at approx. $14.00 retail) in the first shipment, along with the other first 4 books from the collection! If I do not cancel, I will receive 8 monthly shipments until I have the entire 51-book Western Promises collection. I will receive 2 or 3 FREE books in each shipment and I will pay just $4.99 US/ $5.89 CDN for each of the other four books in each shipment, plus $2.99 for shipping and handling per shipment. *If I decide to keep the entire collection, I'll have paid for only 32 books, because 19 books are FREE! I understand that accepting the 3 free books and gifts places me under no obligation to buy anything. I can always return a shipment and cancel at any time. My free books and gifts are mine to keep no matter what I decide.

272 HCN 3070 472 HCN 3070

Name	(PLEASE PRINT)	
Address		Apt. #
City	State/Prov.	Zip/Postal Code

Signature (if under 18, a parent or guardian must sign)

Mail to the **Reader Service:**

IN U.S.A.: P.O. Box 1867, Buffalo, NY 14240-1867
IN CANADA: P.O. Box 609, Fort Erie, Ontario L2A 5X3

* Terms and prices subject to change without notice. Prices do not include applicable taxes. Sales tax applicable in N.Y. Canadian residents will be charged applicable taxes. This offer is limited to one order per household. All orders subject to approval. Credit or debit balances in a customer's account(s) may be offset by any other outstanding balance owed by or to the customer. Please allow 4 to 6 weeks for delivery. Offer available while quantities last. Offer not available to Quebec residents.

Your Privacy—The Reader Service is committed to protecting your privacy. Our Privacy Policy is available online at www.ReaderService.com or upon request from the Reader Service.

We make a portion of our mailing list available to reputable third parties that offer products we believe may interest you. If you prefer that we not exchange your name with third parties, or if you wish to clarify or modify your communication preferences, please visit us at www.ReaderService.com/consumerschoice or write to us at Reader Service Preference Service, P.O. Box 9062, Buffalo, NY 14240-9062. Include your complete name and address.

WPBPA16R